I0699637

THE CONTINUING ADVENTURES OF

Laurel Palmer

BY

PAMELA McCORD

FROM THE TINY ACORN . . .
GROWS THE MIGHTY OAK

www.acornpublishingllc.com
For information, address:
Acorn Publishing, LLC
3943 Irvine Blvd. Ste. 218
Irvine, CA 92602

The Continuing Adventures of Laurel Palmer
Copyright © 2022 Pamela McCord

Cover design by Damonza.com
Interior design and formatting by Debra Cranfield Kennedy

Printed in the United States of America

ISBN-13: 979-8-88528-023-5 (hardcover)
ISBN-13: 979-8-88528-022-8 (paperback)
Library of Congress Control Number: 2022910218

Chapter 1

When I woke up, I was dead. It took a minute for that to sink in.

When it did, I sat up, immediately shooting toward the ceiling twenty-feet above the first-floor landing. Confused, I looked down and saw myself, or what used to be myself, sprawled at the foot of the stairs. I waved my arms, wondering if that's how I would need to propel myself in my current insubstantial form.

Actually, it only took thinking to be able to float down, where I hovered a few feet above the empty shell that used to be me, Laurel Palmer, dead at thirty-two. That was all I'd ever be. I examined the still figure critically. I had been beautiful, hadn't I?

My body was lying there picturesquely, almost gracefully, face up, large brown eyes wide in shock, long sable hair spread around my head like a dark halo. Or I could have pulled that off if my arms and legs weren't bent at strange angles, and a crimson liquid wasn't pooling on the hardwood floor, with strands of that sable hair soaking in it, and my normal olive complexion wasn't unusually pasty, with maybe a little gray creeping in.

I noticed that the filmy silk dress I'd been wearing was halfway up my thigh, fortunately not exposing anything I . . . she . . . might be embarrassed to have on display when the appropriate authorities arrived on the scene. I reached to pull the dress lower, hoping to cover more of her exposed legs, but my hand passed through the fabric.

Floating, both physically and emotionally, I smothered a sob as I scrutinized the body on the floor, fighting to control my skyrocketing anxiety. I had no lingering connection to said body after all, so I should've been able to view it dispassionately. As if. Hand over my mouth, I waited to see if it did anything. Like breathe. I gave a soft, choking laugh. Not likely, since I was *here*, and I would have been *there* if any life remained in the corpse.

I settled onto a step a few up from the body previously known as Laurel Palmer, rested my elbows on my knees, and pondered the meaning of life. Being dead and still here, I mean.

A flash of color caught my eye. Glancing down, I noticed a broken fingernail resting on the step beside me, the ragged edge a shredded mess. Torn off, perhaps, as I grabbed for the railing while plummeting down the stairs? I'd spent a lot of money on those mani-pedis, recently changing the color on my nails to a light sky blue, a color that perfectly complemented the blue hues in my filmy organza dress. Fearfully, I held up my hand to inspect the damage, and felt a brief joy at seeing that all my manicured fingernails were attached.

I was still wearing the clothes I'd died in. No wispy, billowing white nightgown like you might see on an angel in a movie, thank God. I'd chosen my outfit well, not knowing I would be wearing it for eternity. My designer dress and shoes brought a fleeting smile to my face.

Something nagged at my brain, but for the life of me, or make that the death of me, I couldn't remember what it might be. I was suddenly so witty. Unfortunately, there wasn't anyone around to appreciate it.

A worried thought hit me. Where was my husband? Why wasn't he here sobbing over my body and calling 911?

I tapped a finger on my lips. It wasn't like me to be clumsy. I'd never missed a step or stumbled on the stairs, despite hundreds of trips up and down. Never once. Before I could contemplate that further, I heard rustling and thumping noises coming from the second floor. Curious, I floated up the steps and followed the sounds to my open bedroom door, where I spotted my husband, Ethan, searching through my underwear drawer, flinging Natori and La Perla over his shoulder and muttering to himself, "Where the hell did she put it?"

What had he done to our beautiful bedroom? The dresser drawers and armoire doors stood open, contents strewn all over the floor or tossed onto my carefully made king-size bed. A passing thought crossed my mind that he never knew how to find anything in the house, unless it was the TV remote or the expensive bottles of Scotch reverently stored in the liquor cabinet in the butler's pantry.

Narrowing my eyes, I had two thoughts. What was he looking for and, more importantly, why didn't he care that his wife was sprawled dead at the bottom of the stairs?

Unless . . .

Yes, it was possible Ethan had pushed me.

That *bastard*. Why would he push me?

I clenched my hands and swung wildly at him, screaming in frustration as my fists sailed through him without landing a single blow.

A clueless Ethan ran a hand through his short salt-and-pepper hair and pulled his cell phone out of his back pocket, glanced at the screen, and accepted the call.

"April?" he answered, straightening up and sitting on the bed.

I stopped my ranting. April was my assistant. Was she looking for me? If so, she was out of luck.

Maybe I was jumping to conclusions. Ethan loved me. I had been sure of it. There could be a logical explanation for why he was ignoring the body at the foot of the stairs. Surely, he'd called 911 and they were on the way. Maybe he was trying to find my insurance card before they arrived?

I really hoped that was it.

But that scenario didn't feel right. Ethan knew my insurance card was in my handbag which was sitting on the breakfast bar. I watched him smile and chuckle a little at whatever April was saying. He didn't even mention his dead wife lying at the foot of the stairs.

There *was* no logical explanation. My friggin' SOB of a husband had pushed me down those stairs. I knew it in my ghost bones.

Blinking back tears of rage and grief, I thought myself right out of the house by way of the roof, closing my eyes at the exhilaration of suddenly feeling so light and free. I flung out my arms and twirled in the air . . . and merged.

Merged?

I opened my eyes and whipped my head around to see why I was suddenly so weighed down and sluggish, like I'd run into a wall of Jell-O. Probably the green kind.

Hey! a voice assaulted me.

With a jerk, I separated myself from a guy. That's right. A guy. Who was looking at me with the same expression I'm sure was on *my* face.

Watch where you're going, he growled.

My mouth was hanging open, and I used one hand to shove it closed.

He was irritated? He should have been watching where *he* was going. I shuddered at the thought of that ooey-gooey merge thing and fixed my fiercest glare on him.

And noticed something. Hmm. Nice looking guy. My expression softened and I decided to be gracious.

Hi. I'm Laurel Palmer. And you are?

He backed up and crossed his arms as he regarded me. Silently.

I said . . . who are you? He was making me angry.

A slight grin might have flitted across his face as his eyes swept up and down my . . . self.

Wipe that smug look off your face. I could growl, too.

He cleared his throat. *I'm sure this was all just an unfortunate accident. But you should really keep your eyes open when you're soaring through the air.*

I tilted my head, giving myself a moment to consider a reply. I bit back a snarky retort and toned down my irritation.

Sorry. I don't know all the rules yet. I just died. Like five minutes ago. So, you could give me a break, you know.

I'm sorry, too, he replied, dropping his arms and extending a hand. *I'm Teddy Rule.*

Teddy's a child's name, I snarked, then caught myself. Apparently, I wasn't quite over being irritated. *I'm sorry again. That wasn't very nice of me. My unexpected death kind of ticked me off. Teddy's a nice name.*

For a child, you mean? He snorted. *As you can see, I'm well past childhood.* His hand still hung in the air between us.

My gaze moved from his face to his hand. Should I touch him? He was a ghost. Would he be all sticky? As he looked at me expectantly, I gritted my teeth and grabbed his hand, intending to immediately drop it. I was surprised when it felt . . . good. I looked at our clasped hands and back up to his face. And found a glint of humor in his eyes. He squeezed my hand gently and let it go. I felt the loss of his touch immediately.

See you around, he said, and was gone.

I looked right, left, up, down. How did he disappear so fast?

And why was he all Jell-O-y when I collided with him but his hand felt normal? Shrugging, I immediately forgot all about him. There was too much to discover. I devoted myself to soaring through the air, and I twirled and somersaulted and glided for a while until I'd milked all the excitement out of it.

Chapter 2

Growing bored, I needed someone to talk to, to commiserate with, and thought myself to my best friend Kiki's house. She always knew what to do in sticky situations, and this situation was as sticky as it got.

Kiki was lounging by her infinity pool, a tall refreshing glass of iced tea in one hand and a steamy romance novel in the other.

I made a two-point landing on the pool deck beside her chaise, immediately kicking off my Louboutins and dipping my feet into the water. Odd that I couldn't feel anything. Or maybe not, since I was dead. And Kiki hadn't noticed my arrival.

Kiki, you'll never guess what happened to me.

No response.

I jumped to my feet and waved my hands in front of her face. Nothing.

KIKI! I yelled at the top of my apparently nonaudible voice.

I reached for her paperback, but my hand went right through it.

KIKI, I yelled again, then sat down on the edge of the pool, dejected. And concerned. This death thing was going to get old fast.

Kiki used to have great pool parties. I kicked my feet back and forth in the water, which didn't move one iota, as if I weren't even there. How many afternoons had I spent here laughing and drinking with our super-fun friends? Other than my parents, Kiki was the one constant in my life. My very, very best friend for life. She'd always been there for me, and me for her.

And now I needed her, and she didn't even know it. I was scared, to be honest. I didn't know why I was stuck here in limbo instead of going through that door, or light, or tunnel. Whatever was supposed to move me on to the Great Beyond. Why didn't I get one of those? Was it a bad thing that I was still here?

Funny how quickly thinking about Kiki's pool parties morphed into deeper existential subjects.

I did a quick life review hoping to discover what might have caused the guy upstairs to flag my file, but, other than a few cringe-worthy episodes, I thought I'd been a good person. Okay, I was rich, but that didn't automatically consign me to the Great Below, did it? I mean, I gave to charities! Sure, charities hosted fabulous galas where I could wear gorgeous designer outfits and get kudos for my generosity. But wasn't the important takeaway the fact that I was contributing to the cause? And you'd think the time I spent reading to sick kids in the pediatric ward at the hospital would count for something. Because it was real. My heart had wrenched for those kids. I had lost one of my childhood friends to cancer when I was ten and been allowed to visit her in the hospital while she fought for her life. I saw those other sick kids in her ward, with their sunken eyes and pale or jaundiced faces. And I never forgot them, so when I grew up, I often read to kids in the cancer ward and brought them books and toys. I hoped that would go in the plus column.

Of course, I wasn't always rich. Not like I am now . . . or was. My family had a comfortable California life, but we didn't live in Beverly Hills or anyplace like that. I grew up in the suburbs of Los Angeles. That's where I met high school Kiki. We were both on the cheerleading squad and just hit it off. So, that was like, what? Almost mumble mumble mumble years ago? *We're getting old, Kiki*, I said out loud, and sighed. *Well, you are*, I added. I guess I'll be thirty-two forever since I won't be getting any older.

I'm ashamed to admit that we both went to college to meet guys we assumed would have bright futures. And surprise! It worked.

I frowned. Being shallow like that might fall into the minus column.

It turned out that neither of us married our college boyfriends. Kiki married Arnold Butterworth, heir to some port-a-potty thingy. She'd fallen hard for him. It was love at first sight, she said. She met him at an art gallery opening where free wine and hors d'oeuvres were served. We single twentysomethings weren't rolling in money, so we often managed to find our way into free events.

Arnold was an older gentleman, I mean really older, like by forty years, and unfortunately didn't live long after they were married. And when he was gone, Kiki was fabulously wealthy all by herself. And heartbroken. He might not have been Prince Charming, but Arnie was good and kind and completely devoted to my best friend, and she adored him. Despite his age, Arnie was handsome, with a full head of dark brown hair, graying at the temples. Very distinguished. Still turning heads. He was in his sixties but could easily pass for fifty, or maybe even younger. Totally in the acceptable range.

He was trim and athletic, running every morning and swimming every evening, so it was a surprise when he dropped dead of a heart attack. It hit Kiki hard, and I moved in with her for a while to help her deal with her grief until she was ready to reenter the world.

Given her updated social status... from marrying Arnie... we got into exclusive Hollywood clubs and great restaurants. It was in one of those clubs that I met Ethan. He was gorgeous, self-assured, rich. And I fell hard. It seemed he did too, and we were engaged after our third date and married in a glitzy affair at the Huntington Library nine months later.

And then he pushed me down the stairs.

That snapped me out of my reverie.

I love your bathing suit, I gushed as I got to my feet and eyed Kiki appraisingly. *Wish I'd seen it first. I'd be jealous if I could still wear one.* I had to admit the turquoise one-piece looked fabulous on my gorgeous friend, with her blonde hair, golden tan, and long shapely legs. And diamond bracelet dangling off one wrist. She always accessorizes.

Kiki's cell rang and she picked it up. "I forgot the time," she said to whoever was on the other end of the phone. "Just enjoying the pool. It's a gorgeous day. I'm coming back out here when I get home." She listened for a moment." Okay, I'll hurry." She gathered up her towel and her drink, stuffing the paperback under her arm, and headed up to the house. I drifted silently behind as she climbed the stairs to her bedroom. She rummaged in her closet for something to wear out and I lounged on her bed, watching. When she'd moved into the bathroom and started the shower, I lay on my back and stared at the ceiling. I smiled grimly as I thought of something I once read, "*When I was a child, I was afraid of ghosts. When I grew up, I realized people are scarier.*"

In case you couldn't tell, Ethan, I'm talking about you, I said to the empty room, flipping my middle finger at the air.

I popped up and wandered around the room as I waited for Kiki to finish her shower. Stuck in her mirror was a business card from someone she and I met with a few weeks back. I wondered why she'd kept it.

I told Kiki what happened to me while she dressed for her date or wherever she was going. She didn't listen, of course, not even when I got emotional and sobbed into her pillow. When the doorbell rang, she skipped down the stairs and closed the door behind her.

And I was all by myself.

Where was that damn light? What if no one could see me? It was too soon to decide that I was all alone for eternity, but I was at a loss. What does a ghost do? Is this all there is? I floated aimlessly for a time, wondering who else I could . . . haunt?

Chapter 3

I'm just a ghost of the person I used to be. I was so funny with my gallows-adjacent humor.

Out of desperation, I thought myself to my office, my extremely nice office, at Randall Publishing. I was . . . had been . . . Senior Editor, involved in planning and assigning stories to the writers, overseeing a proofreading team, and managing the different imprints we published.

All the busy bees were hunched over their computer screens or on their phones or chatting in the breakroom. The breakroom is where I decided to land. I floated among Beatrice, JJ and Ella, my fellow editors, trying my best to catch their attention. April wasn't around. Maybe she was in the ladies' room. I sighed when no one even glanced in my direction. I sank onto one of the cushioned metal chairs, dejected that I was so invisible. And, to make matters worse, Ella picked my chair to sit on. I shoved at her with my hands, which, of course, went right through her. I thought to slide out from under her, but realized I didn't need to go that route, so I just stood and moved away from her.

She paused, a quizzical look on her face, and glanced around the room.

Can you see me? I shouted, right in her face, but she didn't hear and had already resumed her conversation.

•　•　•

A thought bubbled to the surface. A thought I'd been unconsciously avoiding. My parents were going to be devastated. Before I could blink my way to their house, it really hit home that there was a good chance this might be the last time I'd ever see them happy. Images swirled through my head. The warm hugs and unyielding support and my parents' glowing adoration of their only daughter; the familiar smells of their home that I'd never stopped to appreciate: the fragrance of decades of my mom's cooking and the lingering dusty smell of time. I could picture my mom removing the pan of lasagna from the oven, and I felt a longing that I would never again taste anything from her kitchen. I'd never spend another summer evening in their backyard watching their miniature poodle, Beau, romp in the grass while the sun set. It was all in the past now.

Why do I have to be dead? I shouted to the universe. Thunderous silence echoed around me.

I had to figure this out, to say goodbye, while I still could. In whatever way I could.

Melancholy settled over me as I stood on the sidewalk in front of my parents' house on a tree-lined street in Pasadena. Pink with white trim, so pretty and well-kept, a yard that sloped down to the sidewalk. I could picture my adorable dad in his shirt and tie, pushing the lawnmower around that yard. Don't ask. I could see my mom, standing on the front porch, her hands clasped in front of her, smiling sweetly as I walked up to the door. In my mind, I could hear the way she always greeted me with "Hi, Dear." So many memories of my childhood were wrapped up there.

I willed myself into the family room. Pictures on the mantle caught my eye, and my thoughts spiraled into the past. On the far left was a picture of me in the white-and-red softball uniform I wore in middle school, the huge smile on my face barely visible under a dark batting helmet. The innocent smile of a child who couldn't fathom that her life would end tragically.

The next photograph was of all of us in the backyard of my grandparents' house in Reno. My dad stood at the grill, holding up a hand to wave at the camera while my grandfather focused on the grilling. The grass in their small yard had been a vibrant green, freshly mowed for our picnic, and I remembered its sweet, sharp fragrance. My mom and my grandmother sat on opposite sides of the wooden picnic table. Mom's hair was short, curly brown, her smiling face beautiful. Her blue eyes, the color of a cloudy sky, were always welcoming, always loving, always accepting. There was a red and white checked plastic tablecloth, and paper plates and plastic utensils were stacked, waiting to be loaded with the hamburgers and hot dogs from the grill. I wasn't in this picture since I had been the one with the camera. Back then, I thought I had a gift for photography. With the expected "Say cheese!" I would take impromptu pictures before the subject was ready to be photographed. I wanted to capture the honesty on their faces in that moment of time before the person could strike a pose or force a smile. I forgot that about me. When had I let it go?

I must have mentioned it to Ethan at some point, though, because he gave me a really nice Nikon digital camera for my birthday one year. I often took sunset pictures at the marina, thinking one day I'd print the best ones and create a gallery wall with them.

There was a small picture in a heart-shaped frame of me and my dog, Brandy. He was an apricot miniature poodle, and he was my best friend when I was a kid. I never wanted another dog after he was gone. Even knowing he lived to a ripe old age didn't ease my grief at his inevitable passing. He was irreplaceable. I touched the picture, a sad smile on my face.

And so I turned to go into the kitchen to see my parents again. Hoping to find some way to let them know I was here, that I was with them. That I loved them and would always love them. I felt like I must be shaking, but I wasn't. I was just a weightless thing in a timeless eternity.

Standing just outside the doorway, reluctant to go in as my heart broke and tears threatened to fall, I could hear familiar sounds of them in the kitchen, newspaper rustling, dishes clinking. I pictured the scene in my head and closed my eyes. Overcome with emotion, I could feel the tears running down my cheeks. I didn't know if I was brave enough to go into that room. All I wanted to do was give up. Let go. Fade into oblivion. But no matter how hard I tried to move on, I was still there.

Mom was bustling, cleaning up the breakfast dishes, and Dad was reading the paper at the table, cup of coffee never far away.

I held my breath and moved into the middle of the kitchen, hopeful that someone would notice me, but no one paid any attention to the apparition in their midst. My mom picked up the coffeepot and passed right through me as she refilled my dad's cup.

An involuntary *Oh* slipped out of my mouth, but she neither heard me nor was aware she was standing in the middle of her daughter.

Mom, I sobbed. It was strange. I thought I had distanced myself from the physical world. Emotionally, I mean. But the emotions really hit me when I thought about the phone call they'd be receiving in the not-too-distant future informing them of the death of their only child. I wished I could protect them from the heartache that was about to shatter their lives.

I moved from one to the other and gave each a soft kiss on the cheek. My father twitched his shoulder, and my mom glanced wistfully out the window, each vaguely aware of *something*.

Mom, I called, and, once again, *Mom*. Neither she nor my dad looked in my direction.

I heard the tick, tick, tick of dog claws on the wooden floor announcing Beau's arrival in the kitchen. I smiled and bent down to touch him. He skidded to a halt in the doorway, a low growl rumbling in his throat. My hand flew to my mouth and tears started again in my eyes. *Beau, it's me*, I said, my heart breaking that he could see me but viewed me as a threat.

"Stop that, Beau," my mother said. "What's gotten into you?" She scooped him up in her arms, but his eyes never left me, and his growl grew louder.

Oh, Beau, I moaned, and fled the kitchen.

Would anyone be able to see me? I'd thought Kiki was my best bet, but she'd been oblivious to my presence, and the realization dawned on me that I was alone.

I wanted to scream out, *There's a ghost here. A lonely, heartbroken spirit. The ghost of everything that could have been and never was.* I'd read that somewhere, and it seemed appropriate.

Chapter 4

I let myself drop down through the clouds into the most peaceful place I could think of, the park at the end of High Street. Aerie Park was the name of the magical place I'd loved since my first visit to the sprawling, tree-filled twenty-acre paradise. Fragrant flowers grew in profusion in manicured gardens and in wild areas. Weathered ivy-covered brick walls with wrought-iron gates protected the grounds without denying entrance to people who wanted to enjoy the serenity. I stood on the banks of a picturesque stream gazing into the softly lapping water and sat on a white stone bench in the shade of a spreading maple, tilting my face up to the breeze ruffling the leaves above my head.

I felt drawn to this place. Not that I didn't want to be here, but it seemed important for some reason I couldn't fathom. And it was the perfect place to think. I doubted that anyone living would be able to feel my presence.

The sky wasn't filled with other spirits flitting through the clouds, so there was no one I could ask what I was supposed to do. I closed my eyes and contemplated the universe, hoping an answer would effortlessly spring forth to lead me on my path into the great unknown. As I pondered my seemingly limited options, I remembered the business card in Kiki's mirror, and a name popped into my head: *Madam Rosalind, Medium.*

My eyes flew open. Could it be that simple? For a lark, Kiki and I had booked an appointment with Madam Rosalind for a reading a month ago, not that either of us believed in the hocus pocus. It was just meant to be fun. Roz was a sight to behold. Bangles up and down both arms, flaming red hair held back with a brightly colored silk scarf, long flowing gypsy skirt, the look completed with the requisite crystal ball. Kiki and I had a laugh on our way home because Roz was right out of central casting.

If she'd been a medium worth her salt, she might have given me a heads-up. Some psychic, she was. But, since she claimed to have a direct line to the afterlife, I supposed it couldn't hurt to pop in on her and see what she could see.

Kiki had driven that day, but just because I didn't pay attention to how we got there didn't mean I didn't know how to find the shop.

I thought myself there, landing in the shop's front room. Glass cases offered a collection of crystals and those little pewter medieval trinkets usually found at Renaissance Fairs. There was a red velvet settee and a brocade wingback chair, but no one was sitting in them, and no one was in the waiting area. I heard Yanni-type music wafting from behind beaded curtains which covered the doorway leading back to the place where the magic happened.

I stuck my head through the beads, not even causing them to jangle, but was hit with a loud shriek, and I became aware of Madam Rosalind staring right at me, big-eyed with a hand over her mouth. And a startled client, whose eyes followed the direction of Roz's gaze, but I could tell from her confused expression, she couldn't see me.

Roz quickly threw a cloth over the crystal ball sitting in the center of the round table where the medium did her thing. Her voice shaking, she told her client that the reading was over and the client must leave immediately. Roz mumbled something about evil spirits trying to come through and promised to finish the reading at another time. The confused middle-aged woman who'd hoped to get a lock on her future looked around fearfully and then, ugh, hurried right through me. I needed to stop standing in the flight path.

I turned from watching the client rush from the store to find Roz still standing and staring.

So, um, you can see me?

Roz clutched her throat and opened her mouth, but nothing came out.

I snapped my fingers in her face. *Roz? You in there?*

That seemed to bring her out of her trance, and she backed away from me until she hit a sideboard with her hip and rattled the china cups and saucers sitting on it.

Apparently, you didn't see this coming, I swept my arm up and down to indicate my current state. I waited for her to respond, but it seemed the cat had got her tongue, so I slipped onto the chair the client had just vacated and stared back at Madam Rosalind until her eyes returned to normal size and no longer reflected the fight-or-flight conundrum.

"Wha-what do you want?" she croaked out.

I don't know. I don't know anything about the situation I find myself in. I waited.

She crab-stepped toward the table, glancing between me and the beaded doorway.

Tentatively taking a seat on the edge of her chair, she reached out a hand and waved it through my . . . self.

That's just rude, I bristled. *Are you telling me you've never seen a ghost before?*

"Well, ah, no. No, I haven't."

Wow. Truth in advertising and all that, huh?

Roz sighed heavily and looked less frightened and more perturbed. "So, sue me."

Roz had bounced back. Yay, Roz!

I crossed my arms and leaned forward. *Can you help me or what?*

"Help you what? You're dead!"

Oh, well, duh. Points for you, Captain Obvious.

"How would I know anything about you? I've never seen you before."

That's so not true. I leaned even farther across the table. *Take a good look. My friend Kiki and I came to see you for a reading a month ago. I mean, how busy can you be that you can't remember a customer from four weeks ago?*

Roz tapped her finger on her chin. "Now that you mention it . . . ."

For the record, you didn't do a great job with our readings. Generalize much?

"My clients love me. I'm sorry if you didn't think you got your money's worth, but perhaps you haven't given it enough time for my predictions to come to pass."

Again, I swept my arm down the front of my body. *You didn't mention this. Kind of important. In fact, you said I was going to get pregnant and have twins. I can assure you that particular prediction will not be coming to pass.*

Not making eye contact, Roz adjusted her scarf, which had gone askew when she bumped into the sideboard. "Look. If you want a refund—"

A refund? Are you kidding *me? Where am I going to spend it?*

Roz made the universal settle down motion of hands patting air and slid farther back in her chair, like she'd decided to stay.

She glanced at me from across the table. "Can we start over? You tell me what you need from me, and I'll see if I can help."

Thank you.

"But you have to be patient. This is all new to me." She held up a hand when she saw the look on my face. "Everyone has to make a living."

Huh. I'm surprised you're not that flabbergasted at seeing your first ghost.

"Well, I am, but—" She waved her hand. "What do you want me to do, throw a party?"

You're a tough one, Roz.

She waved her hand again, this time in dismissal of my surprise at her nonsurprise. She leaned back and crossed her arms. "So. Tell me everything. What happened to you?"

I'm pretty sure my husband pushed me down the stairs.

"What? That's awful!"

You're telling me? The rat bastard.

"Why would he do that?"

*I don't know. I mean, I thought we were happy, but—*I stopped midthought.

"But what?"

There's something I need to remember. Something important, but I don't know what it is. Maybe it has something to do with that.

"Maybe that's why you're still here instead of crossing over," Roz said.

Is that what normally happens?

"I don't know. You're my first real ghost."

Whatever. You're the only person who can see me, so you have to help me figure it out.

"What can I do? I don't know anything about you or your life." Roz glanced away and added under her breath, "*and I don't want to know.*"

I glared at her, but I understood. *Look. I realize this isn't ideal, but I don't know what else to do.*

Suddenly, an idea popped into my head. *You can tell Kiki about me, and I know she'll want to help. Call her. Right now.*

"I don't know any Kiki and I don't have her number," Roz said.

Kiki's my best friend. I'm sure if you think back, you'll remember.

I could see she was getting irritated. Any fear she'd initially felt had been replaced by a strong desire to wash her hands of me. Not gonna happen.

Write this down. I rattled off Kiki's number once Roz dragged herself to her feet to find something to write on, muttering to herself and shaking her head in a what-have-I-gotten-myself-into gesture.

Now call her.

"She won't know who I am. What am I going to say to her?"

Tell her to get over here right now. Oh, and tell her I'm dead and she should send the police to my house before Ethan disposes of my body.

She closed her eyes and breathed deeply in a *good grief* kind of way, punched in Kiki's number, and hit speaker.

The phone rang once, twice, three times, and Roz started to end the call, but I told her Kiki might be busy and it could take her a minute to grab the phone, so Roz pasted a long-suffering look on her face and let it keep ringing.

Even I was about to give up after eleven rings when I heard a breathless "Hello."

Kiki! I yelled. *Thank God.*

"Is someone there?" Kiki asked. I forgot she couldn't hear me. So, I waved at Roz to get her to speak.

"Ms . . . um . . . Kiki?"

"Who is this?"

"I'm Roz, or you might remember me as Madam Rosalind."

There was silence on the phone for a moment, then, "Um, okay? What's—"

I glared at Roz, and she burst forth with, "Listen. I have a message from your pal . . . what was your name again?"

Laurel. Laurel Palmer.

"Laurel Palmer. She's been killed and you should send the police to her house right away."

I could almost see Kiki looking at the phone like the caller was insane.

Roz continued, "Her husband pushed her down the stairs and she's worried he'll try to hide the evidence."

"First of all," Kiki said, "how do you know she's dead? And if she *is* dead, how are you talking to her?"

"Hellooo. Medium here." Roz shook her head like my friend was an idiot. She looked at me and I waved at her to keep going. "Anyway, I know how this sounds, but Laurel is sitting across from me right now and she wants you to come here after you call the cops because she needs your help."

"Well, I don't know what to think. I seriously doubt everything you're saying."

I waved my hands at Roz to get her attention. *Tell her not to mention to Ethan that she knows he pushed me.*

"Um," Roz started. "She said do *not* tell Ethan that you know he killed her. Or," Roz glanced at me and held up a finger, "you might be next."

"I should call the cops on *you*," Kiki said, her voice thick with anger.

"No, no, no. You don't want to do that. Can you at least go to her house and see for yourself? I don't think she's been dead that long, so she's probably still on the floor there."

Tell her to take Mike with her, just in case. Mike was Kiki's current fling. And he was a doctor. Not that he would be much use in my condition.

"She said to take Mike with you."

"Are you a stalker or something? How do you know about Mike?"

"I *told* you. Laurel is sitting right here. She told me."

"Well, if Laurel is sitting right there, have her tell me something only she would know about me."

Tell her to get her nose out of the bodice-ripper she's reading by the pool and get over here.

"She said, um, to get your nose out of that bodice-ripper, get dressed and get over here. I mean, she said you're by the pool."

Momentarily speechless, Kiki responded that it was a lucky guess.

Kiki! Oh my God! Of course, she couldn't hear me, but Roz caught my drift.

"Look, Kiki, Laurel's getting perturbed with you. I'm the only one who can see her, so she wants you to come over here so I can interpret for her. This should be easy to prove. Go to her house and see what you see."

"I don't know," Kiki vacillated.

And tell her not to go without Mike. Or some other buff guy, just in case.

"Laurel says to *not* go over there without bringing Mike or another tough guy with you."

"Ask *Laurel* what we did in Palm Springs last month," Kiki said, stalling.

We weren't in Palm Springs last month. We haven't been to Palm Springs in three years.

"She said you weren't in Palm Springs since you went three years ago. Is that enough proof or do you want to keep playing Twenty Questions?"

Big Kiki sigh. "Give me a break. This is weird, okay?" I could hear her fidgeting around, probably getting all her stuff together to go back up to the house. "Oh, all right. I'll go over there."

And tell her to come here after. Tell her the address is stuck in her bedroom mirror.

"Laurel says to come here after you go to her house and call the cops. She said you can find my address on the card stuck in your bedroom mirror."

"Is Laurel really there?"

I could tell when Kiki finally got it, and I let out my breath.

"She is and she's very relieved you finally believe it. Hurry up. And be careful."

Roz put her phone down and waited. Apparently for me to apologize or something.

I rolled my eyes and looked toward the ceiling. *Thank you, Roz*, I said. *You did good.*

"Well," the growing-snippier-by-the-minute Roz responded, "anything to get this over with and you on your way."

I could be snippy, too. *Don't count on it. You're the only one who can see me, so you have to be my go-between with Kiki.*

"Whatever." She stood and disappeared through the beaded curtains. I floated after her.

"You owe me for chasing my client off," she said.

You want me to pay you in ghost money? Cause that's all I got.

It didn't really benefit me to make her angry. I might need her to stick around for a while. A long while.

Roz, could we have a truce here? I know you're a little put out by me showing up—

"Ya think?" she glared at me over her shoulder.

I suppose I'd feel the same way under the circumstances, I conceded. I decided to plead. *But I really need you. You're like a lifeline. You* are *a lifeline. If you refuse to help me, I don't know what I'll do.*

Chapter 5

I started with pretend tears, but they turned real surprisingly fast. Everything hit me at once: being dead, Ethan pushing me down the stairs, nobody (except Roz) being able to see me. No heaven in sight. Why was I stuck here?

Roz stared at me in alarm and attempted to hand me a tissue before realizing I couldn't take it and left it on the table instead.

Dropping her head, she shifted her feet, as if contemplating something. After a moment she looked me in the eye. "So, I have to ask. What's it like?"

I gaped at her. *Being dead? It's shocking. What do you think it's like?*

"If I knew, I wouldn't ask."

I tried to stare a hole right through her, but she didn't back down right away. When I didn't respond, she said, "I'm sorry. I didn't mean to be insensitive. But it's such an obvious thing to ask. You don't have to answer though."

Her apology seemed sincere, and I thought about it. I would probably ask the same thing. Actually, I would probably run screaming from the room.

Roz was about to walk away when I said, *It's awful. No one can see me. I can't talk to anyone, present company excepted. I guess you could say it's incredibly frustrating. And I can't help thinking about what the news of my death will do to my parents. And it only happened this morning, so ask me again in a week.*

"Really? This morning?"

Yes. I've already been to Kiki's, to the office, to my parents'. None of them knew I was there. That's why I came here. You're my only hope.

"That's a lot of pressure to put on someone who hardly knows you."

I know, but what other choice do I have?

After a final look at me, she busied herself around her shop, and I browsed, poking my nose in everywhere. I asked her about something now and then, but she mostly did her best to ignore me as she worked on her books or tidied up or picked up her purse.

Picked up her purse? I freaked out. *Where are you going? You can't leave me. You have to be here for Kiki!*

"Get a grip, ghost," she said. "I'm going to the deli next door to grab a sandwich. Geez! I'm helping you, so get off my back."

You're coming back?

"Of *course* I'm coming back. But I'm still alive, so I have to eat. Is that okay with you?"

I waved her off, then sank onto the settee and laid my head against the back of it. I wished I had a clue why I was still here.

So far, it had been an eventful first day of being dead. And it wasn't over yet. I had to wonder what tomorrow would bring.

Chapter 6

Roz was slightly mollified after she finished her sub sandwich. Not so prickly, thank God. We'd both have to work at this relationship.

Where was Kiki? Had she changed her mind? Had Ethan done something to her? When the afternoon wore on with no sign of my best friend, I got more and more frantic. Maybe I should just go find her, see if she needed help. Not that I could provide any.

As I was making up my mind to track Kiki down, Roz must have noticed how agitated I was and finally took pity on me. "Don't worry. She'll be here. She's probably tied up with the police."

I supposed that made sense. I mean, there was a body at the bottom of the stairs, after all.

The little bell over the front door tinkled and I jumped to my feet. *Kiki! Thank God!* I rushed through the beaded curtains to throw my arms around her but ended up flying straight through her. She shivered slightly but other than that didn't give any indication that she was aware of me.

"Madam Rosalind?" Kiki called. She looked white as a ghost. Heh, heh, heh.

"You must be Kiki," Roz said, stepping into the parlor.

"Where is she?" Kiki asked, glancing around the shop.

"You mean you didn't notice when she zoomed right through you when you walked in?"

"What?"

"She was so excited to see you, she ran to hug you and just barreled through."

"Oh, is that what that was?"

"Yep."

What happened at my house, Kiki?

"She wants to know what happened at her house."

Kiki's hand flew to her mouth and a sob escaped. "It was awful."

Could you be more specific?

"She wants details."

"That sounds like Laurel." Kiki looked over one shoulder and then the other, trying to see me. "I did take Mike with me. Mike's my boyfriend. Anyway, I knocked when we got there, but no one came to the door. Laurel and I have keys to each other's houses, so I unlocked the door and pushed it open slightly and called out a hello, but no one answered. Mike and I went on in and . . . and . . . there she was on the floor. Blood everywhere. Mike rushed to check on her and I screamed, and Ethan appeared at the top of the stairs. 'What are you doing here?' he asked. I said Laurel and I had plans for today, so I came to pick her up. I asked what happened to her and he said she must have stumbled. He said something about the ridiculous high heels she insisted on wearing—"

My Louboutins! I was incensed.

"She wasn't clumsy. She's one of the most put-together people I know. I told him that. I asked if the police were on the way, and he got this look on his face. I told Mike to call 911 and Ethan practically spat at me that it wasn't necessary. He said it had been an accident, so don't call the police, but Mike had dialed the number before Ethan added that he'd already called them and an ambulance was on the way.

"Ethan wanted us to leave. He said he'd call later and let me know what was going on. I told him I couldn't imagine what he was going through, and he said he didn't know what he'd do without Laurel."

I stuck my finger down my throat in a sarcastic attempt at making myself vomit.

"Anyway, as Mike and I were heading to the car, his cell phone rang. It was the 911 operator checking back since Mike hadn't said anything. He handed me the phone and I told them we'd called because my friend fell down the stairs, but her husband said he'd already called and the ambulance was on the way. The operator asked for Laurel's address, and we told her. She had us hold for a minute then asked me to confirm the address. Then she said no one had called in regarding an incident at that address."

Kiki huffed. "Ethan *lied* to me."

That's what she was upset about? God, Kiki! Get your priorities straight. I shook my head, but Roz gave me the calm down sign.

"What happened then?" Roz asked Kiki.

"I marched back up to the front door and let myself in again. Mike and I needed to make sure that snake Ethan didn't try to move the body."

Thank you, Kiki.

"She said thanks."

Kiki ducked her head. "You're welcome."

Did the cops come? That girl could really string out a story.

Kiki clutched her handbag in her lap. "When we first got there, Ethan was heading up the stairs. He didn't look happy to see us again. I asked him how long ago it happened, and he said he'd just found her a few minutes ago. Well, I've watched enough CSI to know that it . . . she . . . had been there awhile. I mean, the blood on the floor was starting to congeal."

Roz looked suddenly sick, the color draining from her face.

"Anyway, Ethan was yelling 'You have to go,' as he made his way down the stairs. When he got to the bottom, he looked like he didn't know how to get around Laurel's body without stepping in the blood, but he hopped over her and said to get out. That he'd clean it up. I said, 'Clean it up?' I couldn't believe he said that. Mike told him not to talk to me that way. He said I was just worried about my friend, and Ethan was saying it was too late to worry about her now. He and Mike were still huffing at each other when we heard the sirens, and Mike and I went out to meet them. There were EMTs and cops both. We hadn't told Ethan we talked to 911 after all. Anyway, the cops asked us a bunch of questions and asked Ethan a bunch of questions. He kept insisting it must have been an accident. He said he wasn't even in the house when it happened. The cops insisted on looking around and sent a couple of officers up the stairs while the rest of us were in the foyer."

Did the cops know it was murder?

"Laurel wants to know if they knew Ethan killed her."

"I don't think so," Kiki said. "Ethan started sobbing as soon as the cops arrived, acting like his life was over without the love of his life. He almost had *me* convinced. I did mention to the cops that Ethan was acting strange when we got there, but I couldn't come out and say he pushed her because, you know, how would I know that?"

Is that all? I was kind of angry that he was going to get away with knocking me off.

"Anything else?" Roz asked.

"Oh. One of the questions the cops asked Ethan was why their bedroom was all torn apart. He said that Laurel must have been looking for something. He said he had no idea why she would do something like that."

Because I DIDN'T! I said loudly enough that Roz grimaced and put a hand over her ear and shot me a look.

He did it! He was looking for something he thinks I hid. I don't know what it is.

"Laurel said Ethan did it. That he was looking for something."

Ask Kiki if I told her about anything like that. Something I wouldn't want Ethan to know about.

"Did Laurel tell you about anything she wanted to keep from her husband?" Roz asked.

"No. I just had lunch with her yesterday and she was in a great mood.

She didn't mention any problems with Ethan."

"I'm getting tired of this," Roz said, hands on hips and addressing me. "I delivered your message. Now you're on your own." She picked up her handbag and set of keys. "Do you mind leaving? I want to lock up."

"But—" Kiki and I said at the same time.

You're the only one who can see me, I said, worry beginning to creep in. *You can't leave me.*

"I can and I will," she responded, attempting to step around me to reach the door.

I flew into her path and glared as hard as I could. *If you leave, I swear I'll haunt you the rest of my life . . . or whatever this is. I'll chase off your customers. You'll go broke.* I put my hands on my hips to mimic her earlier stance.

"What? You want us to be best friends now?" Roz asked, a note of incredulity in her voice.

"What's she saying?" Kiki asked, glancing around the room trying to detect me.

"She's *threatening* me!" Roz said, slamming her bag down on her counter. "She said she'll haunt me forever if I don't keep acting as the go-between for you two."

Kiki giggled. "That sounds like Laurel."

I laughed and held up a hand to high-five her but realized she couldn't see it.

"Do you expect me to sit here all night? I mean, what do you want from me?"

"Well, maybe not *all* night," Kiki said. "I don't want to hang out here all night either. Mike's making me dinner to make me feel better about seeing my best friend's body."

I sank down onto the settee in the waiting room, contemplating being left all alone again. Kiki and Roz were both gathering their things and preparing to go home. I didn't know what I was supposed to do. Stay here? Go home? Wander aimlessly?

As Roz reached for the doorknob, a thought occurred to me and I popped up in front of her, and she stepped quickly back in alarm.

"Do you have to do that?" she snapped at me.

How is this supposed to work? I asked.

Roz looked at me blankly.

I mean, what happens now?

"I have no idea what you're talking about," Roz responded as Kiki watched, fascinated.

Kiki can't hear me, and you can, so I need you to keep me and Kiki connected. So I can make sure the cops find out Ethan murdered me.

Roz crossed her arms and glared at me. "I'm not going to be at your beck and call."

Please? I pleaded. *I'll try to only bother you when I need to. You're all I've got!*

"Well, if *I'm* all you've got, you're in pretty poor shape."

"What's she saying?" Kiki asked.

"She wants me to always be available when she needs to get you a message."

I know, I said. *I'll check in with you every morning, and we can call Kiki to see if she has anything to report, she can tell you and you can tell me. Would that work?*

"You want to pop in here every day? Good grief! I didn't sign up for this!" Roz threw her hands up in frustration.

You kinda did, I said. *You're a psychic, after all.*

"Oh, stop throwing that in my face."

"What's she saying?" Kiki asked, fascinated with watching one-half of the interaction between me and Roz.

"She wants you to let her know what's going on. Through me."

"Um, Laurel?" Kiki glanced around, not sure where to find me. "Like what?"

Kiki, you have to help me solve my murder. We have to figure out why

Ethan was tearing my bedroom apart. What was he looking for?

"She wants you to solve her murder," Roz said, rolling her eyes.

"How am I supposed to do that?" Kiki whined. "I'm not a cop or anything!"

No. You're my best friend and you have *to help me.*

"You have to help her because you're her best friend."

Look, I said. *This day has been surprising for all of us. Why don't we all go our separate ways and think about everything.*

"She wants us to ponder the situation we find ourselves in," Roz said. "Sounds good to me. Now, if you'll both get out of my shop, I'm going home."

But I'll see you in the morning?

Roz dropped her head and sighed. "Fine. I'll see you in the morning."

"Me, too?" Kiki asked, confused.

Roz looked at me for my response.

We'll call you if we need to, I said, and Roz relayed that to Kiki.

And we were done with this awful day.

Chapter 7

Dejected by the events of the day, I had no idea what to do with myself, so I went home to survey the scene of the crime. No sign of Ethan, for which I was grateful. It would have been frustrating for me to want to bash his brains in and not be able to.

The cops and medical examiners had come and gone. All that was left of me was a blotchy red stain on the floor, soaking into the expensive hardwood planks. After sitting so long, the blood would never come out. Oh, well. Not my problem.

My heart clenched a little as I moved through the rooms of the home I'd lived in for the last eight years. I'd loved this house, with its large windows letting in amazing light in all the rooms. The kitchen, a place I treasured, was especially bright and airy. Not that I cooked. That's why God made restaurants. The coffee maker was sitting unused on the counter. I guess Ethan had pushed me down the stairs before breakfast. Crumbs on the table tattled on Ethan's total disinterest in keeping my kitchen perfect. He must have sat there eating toast while my body cooled on the floor in the hallway. I wouldn't even hazard a guess about what an iron stomach he must have to be able to eat after murdering his wife.

Or maybe he had a sandwich after my body had been shipped off to the morgue or the autopsy room, or wherever he instructed it be taken.

I ran my finger over the crumbs. Not one of them moved. I bent over the table and blew on them. Still not one of them moved.

On the breakfast bar, my Fendi handbag lay on its side, its contents spilling out and scattered across the bar. He must have thought whatever he was looking for could be found there. I wondered if he'd checked there first before tearing apart our bedroom.

I shrugged and drifted to the spot at the bottom of the stairs where I'd taken my last breath, staring at the streaky scarlet mess that no one had attempted to wipe up. Squatting down, I touched the stain with my finger, feeling nothing.

It felt like I should mourn this spot or something. Say words over it. But wasn't that what someone else was supposed to do? At my funeral? If I had a funeral. What would Ethan do with me?

Sinking onto a step, I still gazed at the smear of leftover blood at the foot of the stairs. In an instant. That's how quickly everything can change. Just yesterday I was living my best life, and today I wasn't even living.

I'd had pretty much everything. A handsome husband who owned a trucking business, a glamorous job that brought me enormous respect among colleagues in the publishing world, a McMansion in the hills with views and an Olympic-sized pool. A Jaguar in the garage. And friends. I had loads of friends. But none of them came to mind at the moment except Kiki. Thank God for Kiki.

I floated up the stairs to our bedroom. It looked like it had been hit by a tornado. Drawers and doors standing open, clothes spilling out. My shoes . . . my fabulous shoes scattered willy-nilly on the bedroom floor.

Approaching the bed, I surveyed it for a clear spot. Tossed clothing and papers, handbags, hangers littered most of it. I really wanted to lie down, and futilely attempted to swipe the discarded items off my bed. I did mention futilely, right?

I sighed and lay down anyway. I couldn't feel the lumps from the clothes and other items, because . . . ghost. So, I lay back on my pillow and stared at the ceiling.

Do ghosts sleep? So many things I had to learn. I'd ask somebody if I saw any spirits hanging around. Just me, so far. Oh, yeah. There was that cute guy, Benny or something? No. It was Teddy. At the memory, I allowed myself to reexperience the feeling I got when he held my hand. I wondered where he was going. Where he was now. Maybe he could have answered some questions for me. I guess I didn't have to be so snarky with him. I'd try to be nicer next time. If there was a next time.

I could lie here forever. I didn't have anywhere to go, anyone to see . . . or who could see me . . . or any plans for the future.

The thought occurred to me that Ethan could come home and intend to sleep in this bed. Eww. Just that thought prompted me back onto my feet. Until I considered that I couldn't see Ethan sleeping in this trashed room. And I couldn't see him cleaning it up, either.

Oh, right. Dorota, our housekeeper. He'd have Dorota do it. Ethan would want to sleep in his own house. He'd probably have her clean up the unsightly red stain at the bottom of the stairs, too. God, I hated him.

◆　　◆　　◆

Apparently, ghosts *don't* sleep. I knew because I lay on my bed all night and never drifted off or felt the need to drift off. When the sun came up, I was right there to see it happen. Something really out of character for the old me. Now I had to decide whether to get up or just lie there for eternity. That would be boring.

One perk of being dead, I wouldn't have to brush my teeth or wash my hair or pick out something to wear. I am what I am . . . or, more precisely, I am what I *was*. I was thankful I looked my best when I cashed in my chips. At *least*, I'd look good as I went through eternity. Small blessings.

So, what should I do today? I decided to go visit Kiki. I knew she couldn't see me or hear me, but at least it would feel like I was hanging with a friend.

But then—

I felt the need to see my parents. I knew by now they would have received the bad news. They were undoubtedly devastated. I wanted to be there for them. Not that I'd be any help to them in dealing with their grief, but I could stand by them.

So, I teleported myself to their house and found my parents sitting at the kitchen table, each clasping a mug of coffee like it was a lifeline. Their tear-streaked, puffy faces broke my heart. I settled into a chair at the table and put a hand over each of theirs.

They were both looking fixedly at their coffee cups, but my mom sucked in a breath when I touched her.

Mom, I called, wishing and hoping. But she didn't hear me.

My father looked up at her. "Are you okay?" he asked.

"I'm fine. It was just . . . I had an odd feeling like something brushed my hand."

He put his hand over hers and squeezed, and she looked up at him gratefully. And then a tear slid down her cheek and my heart felt like it had been torn out of my chest, and a tear of my own slipped out.

"I miss her so much," my mom said, turning her hand over to clasp his. "She was my baby. How will we go on without her?"

My father just shook his head. "I don't know."

"I should have called more," my mom said. "I intended to call her yesterday but got busy doing things around the house and it slipped my mind. Why didn't I make the time? Now I'll never be able to call her again." She was wringing her hands.

"She knew we loved her," my dad said, attempting to give his wife comfort, even if he had none for himself. "Whether you'd talked to her yesterday or a week ago, she wouldn't have doubted your love." He slipped an arm over her shoulders and pulled her close, letting her sobs soak into his shirt.

My sobs went unheard.

There was a vase of peonies on the breakfast bar, and I read the message of condolence visible among the blossoms. It was from my Aunt Lizzie. She must have jumped right on it for flowers to be delivered so quickly. She was vacationing in Scottsdale or I'm sure she'd have been here with my parents, offering words of comfort. That was all anyone could do. Because nothing helped at a time like this.

My thoughts almost echoed my mom's. Why hadn't I visited my parents more? I mean, it wasn't like they lived in another state or anything. Then maybe this wouldn't be so hard on them. I watched them a few moments longer, wiping away my invisible tears. Of course, it would still be hard on them. No amount of time spent with someone you love was ever enough.

Remembering my mom's reaction when I touched her hand, I wrapped my arms around her. She shivered. Or maybe shuddered. Not the reaction I was hoping for. I wanted her to feel my love, but apparently it creeped her out. Still, I kissed her cheek and she sighed. Maybe she could feel it after all.

I moved to my dad, laid a hand on his shoulder and kissed his cheek, as well. I'm pretty sure he wasn't aware of my touch.

I backed away from my parents. It was too hard to watch their devastating grief. I glanced back over my shoulder as I floated from the room.

I stood on the sidewalk and looked again at the house where I grew up. It felt like my home, too. Then I sighed and made my way to Kiki's.

She was out by the pool again. Always working on her tan. I used to be out there, too. We knew tanning wasn't healthy, but . . . neither was getting pushed down the stairs.

I slipped out of my shoes, sat on the side of the pool, and hiked my dress above my knees. Dangling my feet in the water, I kicked my legs in and out, not moving the water a bit.

Kiki didn't know I was here, and couldn't hear me, so I couldn't ask her if there was any news, but sitting here, legs in the pool, felt like the way things used to be with us. Kiki always had her nose in a book, usually a racy novel. I preferred to swim laps while she read and then would plop down on one of the chaises and soak up the rays.

A bright idea occurred to me, and I took off all my clothes. I was about to find out if ghosts could swim. And the answer was . . . drum roll . . . not that well. I could mostly skim along the top of the water, but it took a lot of extra concentration to dive beneath it. Somehow, I managed to do it, but once was enough.

I supposed it made sense that ghosts couldn't swim, since nothing I did caused an equal and opposite reaction in the water. In other words, my breaststroke, my dog paddle, my backstroke . . . none of these propelled me even a little. On the other hand, if I wanted to, I could *think* myself below the surface or from one end of the pool to the other. I didn't care enough to do that, however. After trying to touch the bottom of the pool once, I realized it was much more pleasant and much less work to just float on top of the water, and it was also more appealing up here. So, I floated, and the only movement I got was when a breeze rippled the surface of the pool.

Still, it was comforting. I hoped no one came outside while I was naked on top of the water, but then I realized they couldn't see me anyway.

I only had a couple of minutes to enjoy that effortless naked floating, because my clothes were suddenly back on. Apparently, costume changes were not going to be part of my allowed activities.

I was floating with my eyes closed when I sensed Kiki had changed her position. She was closing her book and picking up her towel. I scrambled out of the pool rushing to catch up as she headed toward the house.

She paused in the kitchen to pour herself a glass of iced tea. My eyes grew wide as I watched her savor the tea, which I knew was refreshing because Angela, her assistant, made it. And Angela's tea was the best.

God, I wanted one of those so much! I stomped my foot in frustration, but made no sound, which frustrated me even further.

When Kiki left the glass sitting unattended for a moment, I tried to snatch it, but my fingers went right through. Then, I tried to sweep it off the counter, but my hand went through it. Then, I engaged in energetic karate chopping, but the glass of iced tea sat there innocently ignoring me.

So, I gave up. I probably couldn't taste it anyway.

Kiki went upstairs to her bedroom. When she started to get undressed, I assumed she was going to take a shower, so I floated back downstairs to give her some privacy. I didn't particularly want to see a naked Kiki.

After what I thought of as an inordinate amount of time with no Kiki appearing, I headed back to her room and found her curled on her side, peacefully napping.

How could she nap when her best friend had just been murdered? Shouldn't she be all up in Ethan's face, or at least sad that I was gone? I pinched the bridge of my nose and shook my head. And sighed. It just wasn't right.

Okay, I knew there wasn't a lot she could do. I was just being petty. And I was bored, so I willed myself back to my house and sat by my own pool.

Chapter 8

It was a hot August day, probably in the nineties, but of course the heat didn't bother me, and I stayed out until I heard the sound of the front door.

It was Ethan. Who else would it be? Rage surged in my gut, and I stomped toward the house. The closed door was no barrier to my ghostly self, and I barreled into the kitchen just as he set his briefcase down on the breakfast bar and pulled his favorite Scotch out of the liquor cabinet and poured himself an ample amount.

I started to grab the glass from his hand but stopped myself since it wouldn't work anyway. Instead, I simply followed as he carried his drink into the family room and sank into the hunter green leather club chair that was his favorite spot in the house.

Pacing back and forth, I glared as if I could shoot lightning bolts out of my eyes. My murderer had no idea of the angry energy directed his way. Tiring of the pacing, I parked myself on the matching leather sofa and continued to watch the man who stole my life.

There must be some reason I was stuck on this plane instead of going into the proverbial light. I imagined the reason might have something to do with why Ethan shoved me down the stairs. It was funny how death made you forget things you should remember. If I followed him around long enough, maybe I'd figure it out.

Time to follow the clues . . .

So, I perked up when Ethan's cell phone indicated an incoming call. He frowned as he answered and listened without speaking for a moment.

Finally, he said, "I'm trying but I haven't found it yet. I don't know where she could have put it."

He was silent again, then, "Get off my back. I know how important this is." He ended the call and slammed his phone down on the lamp table by his chair. "Geez." He ran his fingers through his always meticulously trimmed salt and pepper hair and stared off into nothing for several moments.

I watched as he picked up his cell again. I hovered over his shoulder trying to see the number on his Recent Calls list, but the screen changed too fast. I did, however, see the number he punched in, wishing I had something to write on. Not that I could pick up a pen. I concentrated on the number, trying to ensure that I wouldn't forget it.

He hit the speaker button and set the phone down again.

"Yeah?" someone answered.

"It's me. That prick Simon just called. He's putting a lot of pressure on me. I'm doing the best I can, but she didn't hide it in our room."

"You gotta do better than that," a man's voice responded.

A voice I recognized.

"I'll check out the rest of the house later. I got rid of her. You'd think that would be enough."

"It won't be enough until we make sure nothing can turn up implicating us."

"You don't have to tell me that, but I wish both you and Simon would get off my back."

"Don't take that tone—"

Ethan hit the End button and stood, running a hand down his face. "Assholes," he muttered. He was sweating, and it wasn't hot in the house.

Eye-opening. Jeff Knight was the voice on the phone. Jeff, my husband's business partner. Jeff, who'd been at our wedding. Jeff, whom I'd entertained in my home on multiple occasions.

What was Ethan into that required him to murder his own wife?

I followed him as he began dismantling our kitchen, rummaging through drawers and cupboards.

He swore under his breath, then moved back into the family room, scrutinizing each item in the room as he considered whether it could hide whatever he was searching for. He began methodically looking into and behind every knickknack and book, end table and cabinet, and not carefully. He left books knocked over, knickknacks moved around, and pictures removed from the walls in his search of the room.

I couldn't even imagine what he was going to do to our bathroom.

Is it bigger than a breadbox? I asked helpfully.

I should remember. I felt a tickle in my brain, as if it was trying to access something.

Now I knew what a ghost was. Unfinished business.

Chapter 9

I dropped by Kiki's for a visit, but nobody was home. I considered where she might be but didn't want to dart from hairdresser to gym to mall.

Too many choices. So, I decided to see what Roz was up to.

She dropped her cup of tea when I materialized in her reading room. She glared at me when it shattered on the hardwood floor and the hot liquid spread over the floorboards and into the cracks between the planks. "What do you want now?" she snapped as she popped into the bathroom and back out with a handful of paper towels.

I glared at her back as she wiped up the remains of her afternoon tea.

I wanted to find out what's going on. Kiki's not home, and I thought you might have—

"Talked to your flighty friend? Sorry. Not today." She stood, dripping paper towels in one hand, and the other hand perched on her hip.

I got the feeling she was trying to dismiss me. But . . . sorry, Roz.

I stood my ground until she backed down from her confrontational stance. When it appeared she was more receptive to my presence, I said, *could you maybe call her? You know. See if anything's happened that might be of interest to me?*

Finally, even *I* was bothered by the puddle of tea forming at her feet and suggested she go toss the paper towels.

And? I reminded her when she stomped back into the reading room that I still needed her to call Kiki.

Roz rolled her eyes, a long-suffering expression on her face, and pulled her phone from a pocket of the long purple skirt she wore, paired with an off-the-shoulder peasant blouse, in white, and accessorized with a red and blue scarf tied around her head. She really rocked that gypsy fortune-teller look.

At first, I didn't think Kiki would answer, but insisted Roz let the phone ring seven times. My mom always said seven was the correct number of rings that would let someone make it to the phone. Of course, that was before everyone had cell phones that were probably only an arm's length away.

Roz held my gaze as we passed the six-ring mark, making a small smirk as she started to hit End Call.

"Hello?" a rushed voice said.

Kiki! I shouted. She didn't hear me.

"Kiki? This is Roz . . . you know, Roz? The psychic? Yes. That's right. So, listen. Your friend Laurel is here. She wants to know what's going on with her, um, case." Roz held up a finger to me to wait. "Uh-huh, uh-huh. Give me a minute. I should write that down."

Roz headed to the parlor and returned with a pad of paper and a pen, and sat down at her reading table, shoving the crystal ball to one side. She wrote something down and said bye and ended the call.

She looked up at me, seeming to soften a little. "So, um, your funeral is tomorrow. At Unity Methodist. I wrote down all the information for you." She started to hand me the note, but realized the futility of that gesture, so she pinned it to a cork message board leaning against one wall. "There. I'll leave it for you in case you forget the details."

Roz turned to me like *is that all*?

I didn't react right away. I was freaked out by the idea of a funeral. I'd given very little thought to the fact that there would be one. Well, in the back of my mind, maybe, but I'd had more pressing issues to deal with. Just being dead was a *big* issue. A funeral, more than anything else, made it all real. I hung my head as I dealt with the emotions rolling over me. Sadness, anger, inevitability, fear. Just to name a few.

"Look, sweetie," Roz said, apparently finally feeling a little sympathy for the situation I was in, "do you want me to be there?"

My head flew up as relief (for some strange reason) surged through me. *Really? It would be so great if you could. No one will see me or hear me, or even know I'm there. It would mean a lot to me.* I looked pleadingly into her eyes. *I'd have a friend there.*

"Okay. I'll be your friend for the day."

I wanted to hug her.

◆　　◆　　◆

I said goodbye to Roz before she noticed my eyes had welled up at her kind offer. Geez. It was like I'd never had a friend before.

I willed myself to Aerie Park and settled onto my favorite bench in the shade of the huge old maple tree. The wind sighing softly through the leaves was comforting.

Trying not to dwell on the dark thoughts threatening to overwhelm me, I listened to the rustling leaves and the babbling of the brook as it gurgled just past the maple.

My mood brightened as I thought about all my friends who would be at the service. If nothing else, I'd see who cared about me. Or pretended to.

It occurred to me that maybe I'd be ascending after my funeral. Maybe that's why I was still around. I didn't know how spirit-stuff worked, but it made sense that a person could stick around for their funeral and then go on upstairs. My mood brightened even more.

Maybe this would be a good time to go see everything I've always wanted to see, since I didn't have anything on my calendar until tomorrow.

Or not. I wasn't in the right headspace to go on vacation.

I didn't know how long I sat under the maple lost in thought, but it was getting close to dusk. Curious what Ethan was feeling with my funeral coming up, I willed myself home.

April and Ethan were sitting in the club chairs in the family room, each holding a tumbler of Scotch. What was my assistant doing there? Maybe she came to pay her condolences.

If so, then why were they both smiling and chatting as if—

Oh my God. He's been seeing her!

I should have been mad, but at this point I really didn't care. Unless that was why he'd pushed me down the stairs.

What did he see in her? Other than her double Ds, that is.

"No reason we can't be together now," April said. The little homewrecker was apparently happy that I was dead. Had she been hoping for this?

"Look, babe, this is all so new. I mean, I just lost my wife."

"But you said you didn't have feelings for her anymore." April's face was scrunched into a frown or would have been if her Botox would let it. I flexed my fingers at her, wishing I could scratch her face off.

"Things might not have been perfect," the liar said, "but of course I loved her." He patted her knee. "That doesn't mean I don't love you, too."

April hmphed and turned her back on him, as much as she could sitting in a club chair. She took a sip . . . make that a gulp . . . of her Scotch and set the glass down.

Leaning forward, he took her hand. "We can be together. Just not yet. It wouldn't look good if I was suddenly seen around town with another woman. You understand, don't you?"

Of course, she didn't. Her way was clear now to move into *my* house with *my* husband and take over *my* life. Maybe, however, Ethan didn't mean any of the things he'd told her and wouldn't be in any hurry to make her the next Mrs. Palmer.

Ethan lifted her hand to his lips and kissed it. "You know how I feel about you." His lips trailed up her arm. "I can't think when I'm around you."

Now he was kneeling in front of her, pulling her closer as his mouth closed on hers. "Do you think we can—"

That was all I could stand to listen to. I had no desire to watch the scene evolve into something that ended up in the bedroom. Or the kitchen table. Or the floor. All experiences I'd shared with Ethan earlier in our relationship. I decided to spend the night on one of the chaises by Kiki's pool and willed myself there.

The night was balmy, not that it would have made any difference to me in my current state. There could have been thunder and lightning . . . and hail the size of baseballs . . . and it wouldn't have bothered me.

I reclined and let my mind go blank, a talent I now possessed, and waited for the sun to come up. I had a funeral to attend.

Chapter 10

By eleven-thirty, I was waiting outside Unity Methodist Church. The service didn't start until noon, but I was feeling antsy, or anxious, or something. Besides, I'd get a good look at everyone who came to bid me a fond farewell. I spotted Roz coming up the sidewalk. She smiled discretely and I felt relieved to see her.

Under her breath she said, "How are you doing?"

Not sure. I'm nervous.

"Why? What's going on?"

Well, what happens after this? Does the white light show up and I cross over? I mean, that sounds logical, doesn't it?

Roz pulled out her phone so she could pretend to be talking to someone. "I suppose that makes sense. Do you have any final messages you want me to give anyone for you? You know, in case you do cross over?"

Tell Kiki she's the best friend ever. And tell my parents I love them. And tell Ethan . . . tell Ethan I hope he goes to hell. Straight to hell. Don't pass Go and don't collect $200.

I thought about it a moment, and added, *On second thought, don't talk to Ethan at all. He's a murderer.*

"Yeah. I plan on dodging that one. Listen, we should stop talking. It's bad form to be on your phone in a church."

Can I sit with you?

Roz gave me side-eye but nodded. "Sure. I'll set my purse on the pew next to me so no one sits too close." She sat and did just that.

Before I could take the seat next to her, I noticed my parents arriving. My hand flew to my mouth to muffle the soft moan that slipped out, although they couldn't hear it anyway.

Seeing my reaction, Roz glanced back over her shoulder to where I was looking.

"Your parents?" she whispered.

I nodded.

My heart shattered into a million pieces as I saw the devastation on their faces that my death had caused. My mother clutched a damp tissue in one hand, and as I watched she quietly dabbed at her eyes. My dad put his arm around her and gave her a resolute smile, then she lifted her head and squared her shoulders as she and my dad prepared to bravely face saying goodbye to their only child.

Still standing, my gaze followed my parents up the aisle toward the front of the church, backing up a little as they passed where I stood. I watched as they greeted friends and acquaintances, clutching outstretched hands, and murmuring thanks at heartfelt offers of condolence. I glided up the aisle behind them, and when they had taken their seats, I softly kissed each of them, wishing I could ease their suffering. Instead, I squared my own shoulders and moved up to the front of the church where my casket sat.

I wanted to see how the undertaker had fixed me up. Ugh. I never liked that dress, and Ethan knew I didn't like it. The jerk. It wasn't enough he pushed me down the stairs. He had to make sure all my friends saw me at my worst. Although I suppose being dead is already at your worst.

And, oh my God, that lipstick color! Ghastly. And too much bronzer on my cheeks. I looked like a cheap hooker. I'm gonna kill Ethan.

I chuckled at that.

People were starting to take their seats. Ethan came in and slipped onto the pew beside my parents, making me cringe. I gritted my teeth as I watched him pretend to care that his wife was dead. *Don't touch them!* I wanted to scream at him when he took my mother's hand and patted my father's shoulder. As if my poor parents hadn't been through enough. My heart filled with anguish, and ghost tears gathered in my eyes.

Kiki arrived with Mike. She appeared surprised to see Roz but smiled at her. I'm pretty sure Kiki mouthed "Is Laurel here?" and Roz nodded. Kiki glanced around the church and slipped her hand in Mike's.

Everyone from my office, including April, was in attendance. April had chosen to sit immediately behind Ethan.

If I'd still been alive and found out about Ethan and April, I would have taken a golf club to his car. I would have dumped out all his Scotch. I would have hired a hit man . . . well, maybe not that one. Point was, I would have been devastated. Considering my current state, caring about who Ethan was screwing was at the very bottom of the list of things that mattered to me. Although I wished I could pull her hair.

People began queuing up to view the body. I watched their expressions. Some smiled, perhaps at a memory of me, some smirked . . . thinking no one would see. Some, like my mom, cried openly. I wanted to gag when April stared down at my ex-body and pretended to dab at her eyes. So, imagine how I felt when Ethan sidled up beside her and put a *comforting* hand at her waist and she turned and buried her face against his chest. Pardon me while I hurl.

I watched him guide her to her seat and take his own next to my parents. I settled onto the pew beside Roz and whispered to her (although no one could hear me anyway), *My husband's banging my assistant.*

Roz whispered back, "Do you think she was in on the murder plot?"

No. I overheard them talking . . . in my den . . . last night. She's dim, but she's not a murderer. Now Ethan has to figure out how to not have to marry her.

Roz nodded but didn't say anything.

The pastor took the podium and the room quieted down. I'd always liked Pastor Hatfield. I'd been coming to church here, albeit sporadically, for the past several years. He always had a ready smile for everyone, proclaiming that his "office door is always open" to anyone who might want comforting words from someone who could potentially set them on the right spiritual path. I smiled as he cleared his throat and began speaking to the assemblage.

Pastor Hatfield wiped his eyes. *Aw . . . that's so sweet . . .* and launched into words summarizing my short life, what a good, generous person I was, blah, blah, blah. As he sang my praises, I glanced around the room to see how many people cared that I was gone. I did a double take. Standing alone at the back of the church was . . . Teddy.

Teddy? What the hell was he doing at my funeral?

Chapter 11

Excuse me for a minute, I whispered to Roz, and instantly was staring down the ghost from my past . . . few days.

Hands on hips I glared. *Why are you at my funeral?*

Your funeral? You're Ethan's wife?

This is so weird. He knows Ethan?

What happened to you? he asked, his eyes staring lasers at the back of Ethan's head.

The bastard pushed me down the stairs.

You, too, huh?

Me, too? *Wait a minute. He pushed you down some stairs?*

No, he drowned me. Same result.

I guess. Why'd he drown you?

It's a long story. His eyes finally left Ethan's head and focused on me.

I tilted my head. *Apparently, we've got an eternity. Spill.*

He just stared at me. I grabbed his elbow. Fun fact: ghosts can actually touch other ghosts.

He glanced down at my hand as I attempted to pull him out the door, finally shrugging and allowing me to lead the way.

The two of us . . . a couple of wild and crazy spirits . . . floated over to the park across the street from Unity Methodist and settled on a stone bench beside the pathway winding through the park.

So, who are you and why did my husband murder you? I asked. No need to play coy, since this wasn't a date, and I wouldn't be having sex with him. Oh, wait. Do ghosts have sex?

I pushed my hair behind my ear and waited for his answer.

Because I was getting too close to outing him as the sleazeball he actually is.

Hmm. I wonder why he killed me. I wasn't doing anything like that.

Well, did you have an argument? Did you cheat on him and he found out?

I scoffed at that. *No and no. And, for the record, he cheated on me. With my assistant.*

Did he want to get rid of you so he could be with her?

I don't think so. She was all starry-eyed about their future now that I'm out of the picture, but Ethan was definitely on a different page. You should have heard him sputtering and backpedaling when she said, "now we can be together."

He laughed hollowly. Both of us were at a loss to explain our current state of being. Make that un-being.

Turning toward him, I said, *How did he do it? I mean where did he do it? I mean I'm just trying to picture it.*

He frowned. I guess I was being a little too clinical about his demise.

I waved my hands in apology. *What I meant is, did he throw you out of a boat or something?*

No, but it did happen at the marina. I got a text from a number I didn't recognize from someone saying they had proof.

Proof of what?

Your husband was smuggling South American artifacts. He was in bed with organized crime helping them move product.

Ethan? Really? I had no idea.

He snorted in disgust. *Really. No idea.*

I just said that, didn't I? This is news to me.

His eyes narrowed skeptically as he watched me. I guess to see if I had any tells.

Look. I'm a victim here, too. I'm sorry if you don't believe me. I crossed my arms and turned away.

Yeah, well. We were at your boat. You knew about the boat, didn't you?

If you mean our yacht . . . yes, I did. So? Are you a cop or something?

Journalist.

I guess you poked the wrong bear.

I guess I did. He ran his hand through his hair.

He pushed you off our boat?

No, it was the dock. His partner was with him.

His partner?

Yeah. Jeff Knight.

Hmm, I mused. *So how did they do it? And why are you still here?*

I have no idea. But Jeff sent the text and was waiting for me on the dock. He said he had names, shipping manifests and destinations, everything I'd need to nail your husband. That's when your husband hopped down from the yacht, gun in hand. When I heard him, I spun around to face him, and felt a prick in my neck and my legs immediately gave way. I was still conscious and heard them say there wouldn't be any trace in case they did an autopsy. I couldn't move a muscle if my life depended on it. Unfortunately, it did. Ethan and Jeff rolled me off the dock. All Ethan had to do was hold my head underwater for a few minutes and it was all over.

I looked at him in sympathy. At least, I hadn't had time to worry about what was going to happen to me. Teddy knew. He must have been terrified as the cold water of the marina covered his face and he knew he was going to die.

So, why didn't you cross over? I asked.

Everyone thinks it was an accident. No one knows I was murdered. I can't leave until they do.

I'm no expert, but just how do you think you can prove you didn't trip and fall into the water?

I don't remember everything clearly. Some things I can't quite nail down. And I believe there was someone at the top of the ramp leading down to the dock. I'm sure they saw what happened. I think they might have been taking pictures.

What did this person look like? I wondered what good it would do, since he couldn't talk to him or her anyway.

I only saw them for an instant, but I think they were wearing white pants with a dark blue sweater. I think they had dark hair. I'm pretty sure it was a woman.

Maybe she called the police.

If she did, they would have been there right away. My body bobbed in the water for twenty-four hours before it was spotted.

If they do an autopsy—

They wouldn't find anything. I didn't struggle. I couldn't, so there's no bruising or cuts that would indicate it wasn't an accident, and even if they did an autopsy, whatever they injected me with would have been long gone. So . . . He held up his hands helplessly and sighed.

He glanced at me then. *Why are you still here?*

I shrugged. *I don't have any idea. I kind of feel like there's something I'm supposed to do, but for the life of me . . . pardon the pun . . . I can't remember what it is.*

What do you remember from before you died? he asked.

I scrunched up my brow in thought. Then I tapped my finger on my chin in thought. Then I looked off into space. *You know, I don't really remember anything. I mean, I remember who I was and where I lived, and most of my life, but it's a blank surrounding when I was pushed down the stairs. It looks like we're both stuck here.*

Neither of us spoke for a few moments after that. What could we say?

He shifted so he was facing me. *You wouldn't have been down at the marina that night by any chance, would you?*

What night was it?

It was Sunday around dusk.

That's so weird. I was killed on Monday morning. You just have a few hours on me.

I can see that's fascinating for you, but think. Did you happen to be at the marina Sunday night?

I can't remem—

Do you have white pants and a blue sweater?

Doesn't everyone? I snipped, irritated at being cut off.

No. Everyone doesn't.

I glared for a second. *Yes. I do have white pants and a blue sweater. And I might wear them if I was going to the boat.*

Think harder. Were you supposed to meet your husband there?

I told you. I don't remember.

Well, would it have been out of character for you to show up at the marina if he was there?

Not really. It's quite pretty out there at sunset and I sometimes join him for a drink when I can. It's our special thing.

Could it have been you?

No. Of course not. I'm sure I would have tried to intervene if I'd seen what was happening. I looked away, contemplating. Could it have been me?

Teddy's shoulders slumped. I could relate. It would be equally as difficult for me to prove I was murdered as it would be for him. Maybe Ethan was an evil genius.

Nah. Just evil.

Teddy and I sat side by side in silence. As I started to say something, my attention was drawn to the people filing out of the church.

Oh, look. My funeral must be over.

Just the service part. You still have to be buried.

Yeah. I don't like to think about the part where I get covered by dirt.

You don't, he said. *That's not you anymore.*

Still . . .

My attention was drawn to the sight of my parents huddled together as they left the church. I reached out my hand toward them, then let it drop. I couldn't comfort them anyway.

He stood. *Well, it's been nice talking to you, but I gotta go.*

Wait. Where are you going? You can't just leave.

Why not?

Um, I . . . I was at a loss as to why he couldn't leave. Shouldn't leave. *What if I need to find you?* I asked.

Why would you need to find me?

Well, for one thing, we were both murdered by my husband. I mean, shouldn't we be working together to figure this out?

No offense, but I'm not sure what kind of help you'd be to me.

I hmphed. *Well, I'm not sure either, but . . . but . . . what if it was me on the dock?*

What if it was? You don't remember anything.

Sure, but maybe it'll come back to me. I know there's a reason I'm still here. What if it's to help solve your murder?

He looked at me thoughtfully.

I might need to reach you in case, you know, it comes back to me. Are you going to be somewhere?

Shrugging, he said, *I suppose it couldn't hurt to work together. I guess you might find me lurking around your husband. Or here's an idea, try thinking about me and maybe you'll just know where I am.*

That might work. And vice versa. You can think about me and find me. I spotted Roz exiting the church. *I gotta go talk to my friend.*

I heard his comment as I reappeared next to Roz: *Wait, someone can see you?*

Chapter 12

Roz was startled when I showed up suddenly at her side, but her expression softened. "You okay?"

It's weird to attend your own funeral. Can you believe Ethan dressed me in that awful outfit?

"I didn't think it looked so bad."

That was him giving me the finger one last time. The bastard.

Neither of us spoke for a moment, then I asked her what she was up to the rest of the day.

"I have to go to work," she said.

But it's Saturday, I protested.

"Saturdays are my busiest days."

I thought about that. *You gave up your busiest day for me?*

She smiled wryly. "Don't let it go to your head."

I had to suppress the lump in my throat. *You did that for me.*

Roz shrugged. "Just a momentary lapse. Don't think it means anything."

I shimmied in front of her. *Of course it means something. I think it means we're friends.*

She let out a big sigh. "I gotta go."

Teddy landed beside me and waved his hand in front of Roz' face. *She's ignoring me.*

She can't see you, I said.

Roz narrowed her eyes at me. "Who are you talking to?"

His name's Teddy. Ethan murdered him, too. You can't see him, can you?

"No. I can't see him. One of you is enough."

Can she help us? Teddy asked.

Roz had started down the steps of the church.

I'll talk to you later, I called to Teddy over my shoulder as I rushed to catch up with her.

She glanced at me, and I said, *Can I hang out with you at your shop for a while?*

She shot me a sharp look, then her eyes softened. "You don't want to be alone." She jerked her head in a *come-on-then* gesture.

Before climbing in her car, she paused. "Don't just stand there. Get in."

I slid through the closed car door, taking a moment to ponder how I could pass through it and still be able to lean against it. Like, how was I sitting in the seat and not dropping through it to the ground? It was all above my pay grade.

I didn't say anything on the drive to Roz's, and neither did she. For me, it had been a draining day. I wasn't nearly as detached as I pretended to be.

She parked on the street in front of her shop, and I followed her inside.

"I have a customer in forty-five minutes," she said, and looked sideways at me. "If you, you know, want to talk."

My shoulders slumped. *I don't know what to think, how to feel. My funeral is over, and I didn't see the white light. I'm still here. Am I doomed to wander the earth for eternity?*

Flustered, Roz tugged at the jacket of the sedate skirt suit she wore for the funeral. She didn't even have that scarf tied around her head. She looked . . . almost . . . normal. But only for a moment.

"Wait here," she said. "I'm going to go change."

I sighed deeply, feeling like crying. I didn't know that not going into the light after my funeral would hit me so hard.

I was running my fingers through the bead curtain separating the front room from her palm-reading studio when she bustled back into the room. She was once again straight out of central casting for a gypsy fortune-teller. It made me smile.

Now you look like yourself again, I said.

"Yeah, well, it's what my customers expect." She busied herself arranging her reading area, spreading a red cloth on the circular table where she conducted business and placing the crystal ball in the center, then positioning the chairs so everything looked inviting to the client.

Then she pulled out one of the chairs and motioned for me to sit down. I did, then propped my elbows on the table and rested my head in my hands.

"I don't think you're going to have to wander the earth for eternity," Roz said. "There's just something you're supposed to do. Once your task is complete, I'm sure you'll move on."

But what? I can't complete it if I don't know what it is. I stood and paced, not even disturbing what little dust had collected on the floor. *It's hopeless.*

"No, it's not hopeless. It's just going to take some time. Maybe the answer will come back to you if you're patient."

No one's ever accused me of being patient. I drifted back into the chair. *Laurel Impatient Palmer. That's me.*

"Maybe you can try to meditate," she said brightly.

Once again, no patience. You have to have patience to meditate. That's just not me.

I rested my head back in my hands. Roz reached a hand across the table as if she were going to pat me but drew it back. "I'm sorry, Laurel. I wish I could help more."

She was sincere. What a turnaround! She couldn't wait to get rid of me when I first showed up. Now we were . . . friends? I felt real warmth at the thought. I really needed one.

I know there's Kiki, but she can't hear me or see me or feel me. Much as Kiki was eager to help, Roz would have to do the heavy lifting.

Roz, I have no words. You can't know how much your help means to me. If I didn't have you . . . I felt my eyes well up and lifted the hem of my dress to dab at them.

"There, there," Roz said, getting a little misty herself. "Why don't you tell me about your friend, Teddy?"

Okay, I said, smoothing my dress skirt and lifting my head. *Teddy was following a lead for a story he was working on about Ethan smuggling South American antiques and got caught. Ethan drowned him off our dock.*

"You two have something in common. Your husband murdered both of you."

The bell over the front door tinkled.

"That must be my client," Roz said. She waved her hand at me. "Can you . . . ?"

I took the hint and floated out of the chair as Roz parted the beaded curtain and greeted a woman who was looking curiously around the shop.

"You must be . . . ?" Roz asked of the woman.

"I'm Patricia Herbert," the woman replied, extending her hand.

"You may call me Madam Rosalind," Roz said. She led the woman into the reading room and indicated the chair.

"How may I help you?" Roz asked.

I watched as the woman, who was just past middle-age and over-Botoxed, patted her hair and took a deep breath.

"I was wondering what you can tell me about my future," Patricia said.

Roz put a finger on her nose in a gesture probably meant to signify that she was collecting psychic information on Patricia, then rubbed her hands and splayed her fingers over the crystal ball which was center stage on the table. "Hmm," she said.

"My dating life has really slowed down," Patricia said. "I'd like to know if there might be someone . . . someone special . . . in my future. I mean, I try to take care of myself. You know, work out, diet, sexy clothes. I don't want to give up on men, but is it too late for me?"

"Time marches on, my dear," Roz said in a somber voice as she gazed intently into the crystal ball. "It can steal the roses from your cheeks, but it doesn't have to steal the stars from your eyes."

Then she straightened and stared meaningfully at her client.

Patricia shifted in her chair. "So, are you saying . . . ?"

"Patience. You need to be patient. You're doing everything right. I feel someone is making his way to you as we speak. Don't give up."

A huge grin split Patricia's face. "Oh, my. That's such wonderful news. When?"

"I'm afraid my sources don't give me specifics. Fate will bring you together with your soul mate when the time is right."

Roz stood and extended her hand. "I hope you got what you came for."

Patricia pumped Roz's hand enthusiastically. "Yes. Yes, I did. I can't thank you enough." She picked up her handbag, which rested on the floor beside her chair, and allowed Roz to lead her out of the room. I assumed Roz would be collecting her fee in the outer office.

While I waited for her to come back, I perused some of the reading room's knickknacks, and the cover of a book caught my attention. I reached to pick it up, but my hand went right through. I closed my eyes in frustration. Being a ghost was such a pain.

The title took my breath away. "*Lily Dale: the true story of the town that talks to the dead.*" Oh my God, I needed to read that book and I couldn't even pick it up. What was taking Roz so long?

I paced over to the beaded curtain and stuck my head through just as the outer door closed behind Patricia. Roz spotted me.

"Just a sec. I want to put her check away."

I pulled back into the reading room to wait, my skin prickling.

I groaned loudly.

Roz heard me as she stepped into the room. "Geez! What's got your panties in a bunch?"

I pointed at the book. *This. Why didn't you tell me about this?*

Her eyebrow arched questioningly as she glanced down at the book I was indicating.

"Oh, that. Didn't occur to me."

But it's the true story of a town that talks to the dead, I said. *What does it say?*

"I don't know. I haven't read it. I barely remember buying it."

You have to read it. Maybe they can help me.

"Do you want to go there?"

Yes! When can we leave?

"I'm not going. I have a business to run. Why don't you just think yourself there?

But—

"But what? What do you hope to find there?"

People who can see me.

"I can see you. What do you think they can do that I can't?"

Maybe they've met ghosts who don't remember things. Maybe I could find out what I need so I can cross over.

Roz looked at me like a busy mother would look at a child pestering her with questions. "I don't know if they could help you or not. I suppose it's possible. Why don't you go there and see what happens?"

I don't want to go there alone.

"Don't be silly. What's the worst that can happen? No one can see you? If you need a wingman, why don't you take your new friend Teddy with you?"

Well, I—

I stopped talking. She had a point. If I could talk Teddy into it, then I would definitely go.

I motioned toward the book again. *Can you read that to me?*

She cocked her head and rolled her eyes. "It will take me forever to read it.

Flip through it then.

When she just stared at me, I added, *Please.*

Roz picked up the book and fanned the pages. "A bunch of mediums live there, and you can go from shop to shop to find one you like. Looks like they have a magic tree stump. It's called Inspiration Stump. Just kidding. It's not magic. It's just highly regarded as a spiritual site."

She looked up at me, then back at the book. "There's a forest called Leolyn Woods where they sprinkle the ashes of dead mediums. Apparently, it's a thing."

She flipped to some old-timey pictures from Lily Dale's early days and read the blurb on the back of the book. "They have thousands of visitors every year." She glanced at me. "Of course, they're all alive. I think people are supposed to ask for the spirits of their loved ones to come through, so I don't know how it would work for you."

My shoulders slumped. *Me, neither.*

I halfway dematerialized but stopped. *Roz, what you said to that woman. About the stars in her eyes. That was epic.*

"Thanks. Poetry lives in my soul."

It should be embroidered on a pillow or something.

Something else occurred to me. *You told her she would meet someone . . . was that a guess or did you know it would happen?* I asked.

Roz fiddled with the multicolored scarf arranged in her colorful hair. "Who knows? When she left, she felt better about herself. She had hope. Isn't that what's important?"

Chapter 13

I willed myself back to my house. No reason. Just had to go somewhere. I thought about Teddy, hoping it would cause him to show up, but nothing happened. I tried calling his name, but that didn't work either.

It was getting toward dusk. I should go see my parents, but I didn't think I could bear their grief. A thought came to me as to where Teddy might be, so I willed myself to the marina. And saw Teddy sitting on the dock, dangling his feet in the water. He looked so lost.

He didn't look up as I floated down beside him, taking off my shoes and dropping my feet in the water. He finally asked, *What are you doing here?*

I wanted to run an idea by you.

That caused him to look up. *What is it?*

I just found a book about a place in New York, Lily Dale. A town made up of mediums. I thought we could go there and see if we could find someone to help us.

You're kidding, right?

I gritted my teeth, annoyed at his dismissal of my idea before he even heard me out. *No. I'm not kidding.*

He glanced at me, then back at the water, then back at me. *Why?*

Why would we go there? Well, because of the mediums. Surely some of them would be able to see us.

Unless it's a scam.

Didn't sound like he was warming to the idea. *Thousands of people visit Lily Dale every year. It's been around for, like, a hundred years. What would it hurt to see if someone there could help us?*

Help us what?

Remember. Help me remember what happened and why Ethan killed me. I climbed to my feet.

It's fine. I can go by myself, I said. I was starting to feel sorry for myself. I'd really hoped he'd be on board. It was less scary having a friend go with you when you wanted to find out why your husband killed you.

I bent to pick up my shoes and smoothed my skirt. *See you around,* I said, trying not to sound snarky.

He jumped to his feet. *Wait,* he said, grabbing my arm.

I looked at his hand and back up into his face. *What for? It's no problem. You already know why you were killed. You don't have to help me figure out why I was.*

He reached up and tucked a strand of hair behind my ear. And my heart stopped.

Okay, my heart was already stopped, but you get the picture. I felt a glimmer of hope that I wouldn't be alone in this.

When do you want to go? he asked.

Why wait? Let's just go now.

We'll get there in the middle of the night, he pointed out.

I laughed. *Are you afraid of the dark?*

Pffft. He blew out an *as if* breath.

Hey, Roz said Lily Dale is close to Buffalo, which is close to Niagara Falls. I haven't ever been there. Have you?

Nope. What are you suggesting? He quirked an eyebrow at me. *You want to go over the falls in a barrel?*

Definitely not that, but we could visit before we go to Lily Dale. I think they light up the falls at night. I bet it's gorgeous. I just want to see it. It's on my bucket list.

That elicited a real laugh. *It's a little late for a bucket list, don't you think?*

It's not too late until you die. And apparently sometimes even then it's not too late. I put my hands on my hips and pinned him with a look. *So, you in?*

Yeah, sure. Why not? And we don't even have to pack.

Anything on your bucket list? I asked.

I was too young to have a bucket list. I'm good.

Chapter 14

Niagara Falls is magnificent. Bigger than you can even imagine. And it's lit up with colors that change periodically, kind of like a rainbow, or those color wheels that used to go under metal Christmas trees that made the tree change color. The falls take your breath away. We found a viewing point and stood, billowing plumes of mist soaking us. I would have needed a raincoat if I was still alive.

We weren't alone. There were a dozen other people leaning over the railing, oohing and aahing at the magnificence they beheld. A couple near us began making out after the woman exclaimed how romantic the falls were. I watched long enough to deduce they didn't intend to stop their PDA anytime soon, then tapped Teddy on the shoulder and tipped my head in the direction of the couple.

I guess they're keeping each other warm, he said with a shrug, his attention returning to the breathtaking scene we'd come all this way to see. I barely heard him over the roar of the water and turned to look at the couple again.

I remembered making out like that. Marriage had kind of put a damper on it, though. I mean, Ethan and I were super into each other when we got married but somewhere along the line we stopped being so . . . demonstrative. I remembered the feeling of almost melting into the other person and the incredible high of magical kisses. I didn't realize how much I missed it.

I glanced at Teddy and back at the couple, who had finally moved on to gazing into each other's eyes, then back at Teddy.

Hmm, I thought. Do ghosts kiss? If I were alive, I'd definitely be thinking lascivious thoughts about him. Assuming I was single.

I leaned up on my tiptoes and whispered his name in his ear, and he looked down at me. *What the hell*, I thought and pulled his face down to mine. He stiffened for an instant, but only for an instant, before his arms went around me and suddenly we were entwined. And I have to say, ghost lips feel *fine*.

We didn't stay lip-locked as long as the subject couple, but it was a substantial, heart-stopping make-out session.

Then it was over, and both of us were embarrassed.

What was that about? Teddy asked.

I tried for a nonchalant, *It looked like fun*, but I was sure if I wasn't transparent I'd have been bright red.

I tossed my hair and said, *Ready?*

Ready? he asked, as if he thought I meant we should get naked and do it right on the spot.

Not for that. *Good grief! I meant are you ready to go to Lily Dale?*

He rolled his eyes. *Sure.*

I snuck a glance at him, grabbed his hand, and wished us to Lily Dale.

We touched down in front of the entrance, which featured a large metal archway proclaiming "Lily Dale Assembly."

I was in awe. With dawn just starting to break, the place was lovely. A forest wonderland. I started to twirl around, forgetting I was still holding Teddy's hand, and it pulled me up short. I apologized and let go, then scampered off toward the quaint Victorian houses that made up Lily Dale. The town is near Cassadaga Lakes, and mist was rising off the water and weaving among the trees, a sight that almost took my breath away. SoCal girl here. Never did any camping either. The only mountains I was familiar with were in Aspen and Lake Tahoe when they were covered with snow.

Although, technically, Lily Dale was in a forest and not a mountain. Semantics.

The town was starting to wake up, and lights were coming on in some of the houses. We had a little time to explore before confronting the mediums with our plight.

Spotting a sign that said "Fairy Trail," I pointed it out to Teddy and together we wandered down the path. I think this was a really old forest. I'm not totally up on my horticulture, but I recognized pines, red oaks, maples, and didn't recognize a ton of other tree varieties. I'm sure there would be a heavenly aroma if I could still smell. The Fairy Trail was full of delightful surprises. Small ceramic and plastic fairy or gnome figurines were hidden among the trees and plants, and here and there were tiny fairy houses and fairy towns if you looked hard enough to find them.

I was delighted.

We wandered back to town and found benches arranged facing a stump. I thought it odd until I remembered Roz telling me it was magic or something. Inspiration Stump . . . that was it. I related what very little I knew about it to Teddy as we sat on a bench in the front row.

They do medium stuff here, I said. *Feel anything?*

We both looked around. It felt alive, like it should be teeming with spirits, but neither of us saw anything.

I think other spirits are here, I said, *but I don't know why we can't see them.*

Maybe we can only see each other because we're connected somehow, Teddy said. *Because of Ethan?*

Or maybe they have to want to let us see them? Still don't know all the rules.

So. Teddy looked at me and quirked an eyebrow.

I gulped. *So, what?* I asked, playing innocent.

Don't you think we should talk about it?

About what?

That you kissed me.

Dang. I so hoped he wouldn't bring that up. I dropped my head, my hair falling forward to obscure my face. My red face. It felt red anyway.

You didn't seem to mind. I got all huffy.

I didn't say I minded. I'm just confused about why you did it.

I tossed my head back and rolled my eyes. *I just wanted to, okay? I mean, I was curious what all we can do as ghosts and wondered what it would be like to kiss one. You. Kiss you.*

The corner of his mouth turned up. *And what was it like?*

God. He wasn't going to drop this. *It was okay.*

Just okay?

I crossed my arms and turned my back on him. I was confused, too. I didn't know why I did it.

He waited silently and, after a minute, I turned back to him. *You know, that other couple that was making out. I remembered how much fun it was. And you're not bad to look at . . .*

He full-on grinned. *You're not so bad yourself.*

I smiled up at him. Feeling a little less alone.

He lifted one of his arms and looked at me expectantly. I found gentleness in his eyes, and snuggled under his arm with a soft sigh.

We sat like that, together, until the denizens of Lily Dale started bustling about their day.

I wasn't sure what I was feeling about Teddy. It was weird, like we were a couple or something. Or a couple *of* something. I had to admit that it felt good having his arm around me.

I was curious about him. I didn't know where we would go from here, but it seemed like we might go there together.

I ducked from under his arm after a while and he looked at me questioningly. I twisted a strand of hair around my finger as he watched me. Finally, I glanced at him from under my lashes.

Did you, um, leave anyone behind?

His face registered surprise and he didn't answer right away. Then he said, *Not really. My parents are gone, and I broke up with my ex six months ago.*

Ex . . . wife?

No. Ex-girlfriend. The only important thing I left behind was Buck. My dog.

Oh, no! He'll starve!

He's fine. My best friend Link went over and got him as soon as he heard about my death. I checked up on them once. Of course, Link didn't know I was there. I'm not so sure about Buck. I swear he lifted his head and looked at me.

I nodded meaningfully at his arm, and he allowed me back under it. *I know what you mean. I visited my parents after I was . . . I was . . . deceased. They have a poodle named Beau, and Beau could see me. And he was freaked out, barking and growling. It hurt my feelings. I've known him almost his whole life.*

I sighed. *It was hard, seeing my parents. I visited them again after they were notified. Their grief was so deep, so real. I wish so much they had been spared having to go through that. I wish it even more than I wish I hadn't died. I could barely deal with the sadness.*

He reached up and ran his fingers through my hair. I hadn't felt so taken care of in forever and I let out a small, contented sound.

He tilted my chin up and kissed me, and I melted into him. Then he touched my hair again and I ducked back under his arm, my arm circling his waist.

After another few moments, I said, *What are you bummed about missing now that you're dead? What do you most regret not having the chance to do?*

I don't know, he said. *I suppose that I'll never have kids. Not that I was ready, but I always thought I'd be a great dad.*

I smiled. *You would have been. I can tell.*

What about you? he asked.

First of all, I didn't really have a bucket list. Just so you know. I tilted my head back so I could look up at him. *I wanted kids, too.* I was embarrassed when a ghost tear slid down my cheek and I reached a hand up to brush it away. *Look at us, feeling sorry for ourselves*, I said.

A deep grief washed over me. *Don't*, I said sharply. *Don't*, I repeated more softly.

Don't what? a clearly confused Teddy asked.

Up until this minute, I thought I'd been dealing quite well with my death and current ghostly situation. That would have been too easy, wouldn't it? Suddenly I felt a flood of emotions that threatened to swamp me. Anger, sadness, anxiety, fear, and . . . grief. Grief for myself. That one ghost tear released a torrent that I was afraid would never stop.

As if understanding, Teddy engulfed me tightly in a hug, kissing the top of my head.

It'll be all right, he said.

His words were comforting, but would it? Would it really be all right? I wiped at my tears, which weren't really there, and said, *Thanks.*

He held me a minute more, then asked, *Are you okay?*

I'd never been a doom and gloom person. More like perpetually sunny. And, if this was going to be my eternity, I wouldn't spend it feeling sorry for myself. So, I pulled away, sat up straight, and said, *I'm fine. Or I will be fine. Sorry if I scared you.*

He gave a small laugh, then glanced past me. People were arriving and starting to sit on the benches facing the magic stump. I let out an *Eek!* when ample rear ends belonging to two older women headed our way, and we vacated our spot before we became someone's seat cushion.

You know what I miss? I said, as we found other seats that didn't seem in danger of being occupied. *Starbucks. I can't believe I'll never get to have another Vente Mocha with whipped cream. My favorite.*

Teddy laughed. *I'm more a straight black coffee guy.*

I guess we're not compatible then, I said.

Chapter 15

An older woman with long frizzy gray hair and a ton of bangles and bracelets faced the assembled fans in front of Inspiration Stump. She smiled warmly out over the crowd, which probably numbered about two dozen, and clasped her hands in front of her.

"Welcome," she started. "It's wonderful to have you here in Lily Dale. It's beautiful here, isn't it?" She paused to smile and, I assume, absorb the spirituality.

"My name is Evelyn Doherty. We've been holding these services here for a very long time. Since the late 1800s. I encourage you to renew your own spiritual energies. Open your awareness and you might just receive a message from beyond the veil. Now, I must ask you to be considerate of those giving and receiving messages. Too much moving around or talking can disrupt the flow of energy from our mediums and from you.

"Let me introduce you to one of our resident mediums, Carol Barlow, and we're lucky to have Pansy Rivers visiting us here from Virginia. Now, if you'll all silently encourage your departed loved ones to come through, we'll see what happens today."

Carol Barlow, a jovial black woman with a radiant smile, stepped forward and said, "I'm Carol. I've been a resident of Lily Dale for the last fifteen years. I came here as a young woman of twenty-two and never left. The community here is warm and inclusive, and I have made lifelong friends among the citizens of this magical place. My wish is that I can bring hope and comfort to you by bringing you messages from your loved ones who've passed on."

A breathless crowd watched as Carol reached her hands out in front of her and closed her eyes. No one made a sound as they waited to see who would come through.

Finally, Carol spoke. "Geneva is here. Does anyone know Geneva?" She opened her eyes and scanned the audience until an elderly woman stood and said, "It's me! Geneva came for me!" Her hand flew to her mouth and hope glowed on her face. "What is she saying?"

"She says there was an accident. I don't think it was recent. Does that make sense?"

"Oh, yes!" the woman exclaimed. "Geneva's my daughter. She was killed in a hit-and-run accident when she was thirty-one." Her eyes dropped. "That was seventeen years ago." Tears were running down her cheeks.

"Can you come up here, please?" Carol addressed the woman, who made her way to the front of the assembly and stood tentatively in front of Carol.

"What's your name?" Carol asked.

"I'm Antonia," she said, as more tears fell.

"Well, Antonia, Geneva wants you to know that she's fine. She's at peace and she wants you to be at peace as well. She looks forward to seeing you again when you cross into the light." Carol took Antonia's hand and squeezed it. "Can you be happy now? That's what Geneva wants for you."

"Yes! Yes. I'll see her again." Antonia thanked Carol profusely and wiped her tears on a tissue clutched in her hand. She smiled shyly at the audience and made her way back to her seat to a smattering of applause.

Carol asked for quiet again, closing her eyes and concentrating. When she opened them, she said, "Is there an Eileen present?"

A young teen stood and said, "That's me." She looked around to see if there were any other Eileens present.

"Your mother is here," Carol said. "Has she passed on?"

Eileen nodded. "She died two years ago. Breast cancer."

"Your mother wants you to make an appointment to see your doctor. You have a bump on your neck?"

Eileen's hand flew to her mouth. "Yes," she said softly. "Is it—"

"She doesn't want to alarm you, but she said for you not to wait to do this. If you hurry, everything will be all right." Carol looked into the air like she was receiving another message. "And, Eileen, your mother is very proud of you."

Teddy said, *Carol's good, isn't she?*

No kidding. I think she's the one we need to talk to.

Eileen was crying and her companion, maybe a sister, slipped an arm around her and led her away from the gathering.

Carol said, "One more, then I'm going to turn the floor over to Pansy." She glanced out over the audience. "Brenda, your husband's insurance policy is in the middle desk drawer in his office."

There was a gasp from the crowd. "He's here?"

"Yes," Carol said. "He's been watching over you. You need to find that policy. He said he misses being with you."

"Hi, Doug," Brenda called out. "I miss you, too."

Carol laughed. "When did you lose your husband?"

Brenda gulped back a sob. "Only three weeks ago. He slipped on a wet floor and hit his head. I can hardly breathe for missing him."

"I'm so sorry for your loss, Brenda, but please know that he's never left your side. I hope you can find comfort in knowing that death isn't the end of everything."

Brenda managed a small smile. "Thank you."

Carol turned toward Pansy and invited her to come forward. She clasped Pansy's hand and said, "We're so happy to have you here. Good luck."

Pansy was a whole different story. I shook my head at her transparent attempts at giving readings.

She asked for a show of hands of people who wanted to contact their loved ones and picked a slightly overweight fortysomething man out of the crowd and asked him to stand.

"What's your name?" she asked.

"George." The man tugged down a snug-fitting Hawaiian shirt as he stood.

"I feel like someone is trying to come through," Pansy said. "It's a man, maybe a grandfather. Does the letter "M" mean anything to you?"

George's face scrunched up in an effort to think. "Um, not really. I knew a Marty a couple of years ago. He was someone I worked with."

"Did he pass away?"

"Now that you mention it, I think he did."

"Good. Marty wanted you to know that he's doing well."

"Oookay," George said, obviously skeptical. "Except he was a younger man than me so definitely not a grandfather."

"More than one spirit was trying to get through. I guess Marty was the pushy one." Pansy stopped to allow for laughter. "Was your grandfather's name John?"

"No. One of my grandfathers was named Joseph and the other was named Vance."

"Joe, then. He's the one who's coming through. He said he was at your wedding and your bride was beautiful."

George let out an uncomfortable chuckle. "Um, nice that he could make it."

Pansy seemed not to notice that George wasn't getting emotional over a visit from his *grandfather*. "Well, thank you, George." She looked over the audience again. "Anyone else?"

We sat through a few more feeble attempts by Pansy to connect to the spirit world, and possibly try to pull the wool over gullible eyes, and were relieved when Evelyn again approached the front to wrap up the assembly, indicating there would be another one at two o'clock that afternoon.

That was eye-opening, Teddy said.

I hope Carol can help us, I said. *She's the real deal.*

Hopeful attendees clamored for attention as they moved away from Inspiration Stump. Evelyn announced that it wasn't possible to stop and speak to each of them as the mediums had appointments to get to. She encouraged everyone to sign up for individual readings with any of the many mediums who called Lily Dale home.

Chapter 16

Teddy and I followed Carol, hoping for a moment to attempt to connect with her. The crowd had given up trying to talk to the mediums and wandered off to sightsee, so Carol was alone when she reached her bright yellow three-story Victorian house. We entered behind her. She didn't seem to notice us, at least she didn't acknowledge our presence, even as I called out to her. We followed her into another room set up to do readings. It reminded me of Roz's reading room, with a small round table and a deck of tarot cards. No crystal ball, though. I talked, hoping she could hear, but got no response. She was busying herself preparing a cup of tea, her back to us, as if we weren't there. I shook my head at Teddy, growing irritated. Of course she knew we were there.

Why are you ignoring us? I said sharply. *We need your help.*

In frustration, I shoved at the deck of tarot cards, and was surprised when it flew off the table. Carol spun around and looked me right in the eyes.

"I have real, paying customers. I don't have time to solve ghost problems all day long." She slammed her cup down on the table. "And there are ghosts with problems snipping at me all day every day. So be gone with you."

I knew you could see us, I said. *You were so nice to Antonia and Eileen. Why are you so rude to us? Is it all about the money with you?*

"You make it sound like that's a bad thing. A girl's got to make a living, and I have a reading in five minutes. Let me drink my tea before she gets here."

Carol waved her hand around the room. "Don't you see the ten other ghosts trying to get my attention? I can't play favorites."

Actually, I didn't see any of them, and, from Teddy's expression, he didn't either. *I don't see any ghosts. If I can't see them, maybe they can't see us.*

"Your point?"

Carol was just as snarky as Roz. Was it a requirement of the position?

Five minutes. That's all we need. I'm going to keep pestering you until you talk to us. I knocked over her teacup and she jumped up and ran from the room. In a moment she was back with paper towels to mop up the spilled tea.

Teddy, I whispered, *did you see that?*

I did. Could you always do that?

No. I've never been able to move anything before.

Carol glared at us, holding a dripping paper towel in one hand. "You've got five minutes."

Thank you, Carol. I'll be fast. Teddy and I were murdered by my husband. We want to cross over, and it appears something's keeping us here, but we don't know what it is. I can't remember much around the time of my death, and I need to know what happened. What do we do?

"How would I know?" Carol snipped. Then she took a breath and softened. "Seriously, I don't know what I can do to help you. I speak to dead people, but I only know what they tell me. You need a psychic. Or maybe you need a hypnotist to regress you. I'm sorry not to be more help, but there's truly nothing I can do."

Is there anyone here who might be able to help us? I asked.

"Susie Twilight is a psychic. I've heard good things about her. If you go to the end of my street and turn right, you'll see her small green cottage. I'm not sure she's there, but she's your best shot."

Thank you. I'm sorry we had to strong-arm you, but we're desperate.

We left her standing in her reading room still holding the dripping paper towel.

Teddy took my hand as we stepped off Carol's porch, and I didn't mind. I smiled up at him.

Isn't it strange? I asked. *We can touch each other, but remember the first time we ran into each other how mushy it was? Why do you think this is different?*

He furrowed his brow in thought, then said, *I think it's because we're focusing on each other. I don't mean* focusing *focusing, but just that we're aware of each other so we're solid to each other. Lame explanation, but it's all I got.*

I laughed. *It's better than I could come up with.*

We walked in silence for a while. There were people milling around some of the mediums' houses, or sitting on benches in grassy areas, probably waiting for their appointments. Most were serious, although I heard some nervous laughter, and saw some with sad faces, some with hope spilling from their eyes. I thought of my parents and my heart clenched. I wondered if they would search for closure, and maybe find their way here.

But no. My parents were bent under their grief, but not broken. They would grit their teeth and go on living, but maybe the hope would no longer spill from their eyes.

Hey, you okay? Teddy asked.

He startled me out of my reverie. *I'm fine. Just thinking that all these people are searching, grief-stricken and grasping at straws. Anything to connect them with those they've lost. It makes me so sad.*

I know, he said. *Unfortunately, there's nothing we can do for them.*

I know. I squeezed his hand. *I know,* I said again softly.

We reached the end of Carol's street and turned right at the corner. Three houses down was a green cottage and we found ourselves standing in front of a picture postcard of a magical-looking home. It was a cheery green with window boxes dripping with colorful flowers and rose bushes lining the walkway up to the front door. There was a handcrafted shingle out front that read, "Susie Twilight, Psychic Medium." There were two women sitting in chairs on the wide porch. They weren't interacting; each lost in her own thoughts. I glanced at Teddy, and we walked up to and through the front door. No one was in the waiting area, but I heard voices coming from an open door on our right down a short hallway and we headed that way.

I could tell Susie Twilight saw us by the narrowing of her eyes when she looked right at me. I was sure when she frowned and waved her hand to dismiss us. Her client turned to see what Susie was waving at, but of course saw nothing. The psychic mumbled some excuse that seemed to satisfy the woman.

I crossed my arms and glared back at Susie. I could see her jaw tighten as she gritted her teeth. *We'll be in the waiting room*, I said, confident the client couldn't hear me.

Half an hour later the customer left, and Susie confronted us, hands on hips. "You can't be here. I have customers to help. Whatever you want, I'm not interested."

Look, I said, trying for a conciliatory tone, *we wouldn't be here if we didn't need your help. Carol sent us.* Which wasn't entirely true. *Carol thought you could hear us out and see if there's anything you can do to help us.* When she didn't respond, I said, *Please?*

Susie stuck her head out the door and indicated that she'd be with the waiting customers in a few minutes, then glowered at us as she said, "You have five minutes."

What's with you mediums and your five minutes? I glanced at Teddy, then said, *Never mind, I'll talk fast. I'm Laurel Palmer. This is Teddy Rule. We've been dead for about a week. We were both murdered. The cops think our deaths were accidents. We can't let Ethan . . . that's my husband . . . he's the one who killed us . . . get away with it. I guess that's why we're still stuck here instead of going into the light. Which was conspicuously absent at the time of my death. Or Teddy's.*

"Your husband caught you two together, so he killed you?"

Of course not. We never really met until Teddy showed up at my funeral and we compared notes. Then we decided to help each other.

"So, what is it you expect me to be able to do about it?" she asked, sounding a little less annoyed.

We don't know. There must be someone who can help us. My shoulders slumped and Teddy took my hand. *Thing is, I can't remember the time right around my death, and I have a super-strong feeling that there's something I need to remember.* I looked at Teddy and back at Susie. *Can you do anything, anything at all, to help me find out what I need to know so we can cross over?*

"What about him?" She indicated Teddy.

He knows what happened to him. I think whatever I have to remember is the key to releasing both of us. I squeezed his hand. *Lucky for me he's sticking by me.*

She regarded us silently for a moment. "Look, I don't think there's anything I can do. I could have told you where your bodies were . . . I might even be able to identify the killer . . . but it's not like a television crime show. I can't go back and follow you around to see what happened just before you died. I have no way to know what it is you need to remember. I'm sorry." She shook her head. "I really am."

It was a long shot. I just hoped there'd be an answer for us here.

"I wish I had a suggestion for you. I don't know of any of the residents here who would do the kind of . . . investigation you need. If you were still alive, I'd tell you to find a good hypnotist to regress you."

At least you took the time to hear us out. Thank you for that. We'll get out of your way. I gave her what I was sure was a pitiful smile.

Before we could leave, she said, "Wait. I almost don't want to tell you this. It's rare for spirits to . . . team up. I believe people who have gone on to heaven, or whatever you believe is the ultimate destination, will be reunited with those loved ones who've gone on before them. But I don't think I've ever run into ghosts like you, who care about each other and who are on a journey together. It's . . . special. But it isn't going to last, Laurel. I see you alone. I'm sorry."

What? I asked. *Where will Teddy be? Are you sure?*

"I hope I'm wrong, but at this moment, that's what I see." She spread her hands in a helpless gesture. "I wish you luck."

I had a sinking feeling in my stomach as Teddy and I bid Susie goodbye and almost fled from her home. In a panic, I had to get away from there. And I needed to think. Susie Twilight had effectively stripped away the small feeling of being safe that I could hold onto.

I'm not going anywhere, Teddy said, taking my hand.

But she said—

We don't know she's a hundred percent right about everything. I won't leave you.

I wanted to believe him. I did. But a kernel of fear was growing inside me. I didn't say anything but smiled up at him in a way which I hoped would reassure him that I wouldn't worry about losing him.

This sucked.

We walked aimlessly in silence and ended up back at Inspiration Stump and sank onto a bench.

I looked side-eyed at him. *You aren't stuck with me, you know. You don't really have to hang around with me. I know you have your own path and maybe you think you'd accomplish more on your own.*

He slipped an arm around me. *Look, I don't know what that psychic was talking about, but I'm not going anywhere. I think that together we have a better chance of figuring everything out.* He looked down. *I don't want to be alone either.*

I straightened. *We can play it by ear. If you do have to leave at some point, we'll deal with it then. Fair?*

Sure, although I don't expect to leave.

His statement made me feel better. But a tiny sliver of my brain was still worried. When did it happen that he came to mean so much to me? The thought of losing him was like a rip in my soul.

So, what do we do now? I asked. *Since this was a bust.*

It wasn't a bust. We got to see Niagara Falls. And you kissed me.

I would have blushed if I weren't transparent.

Yeah, I said. *Best decision I've made in a while.*

Should we go back? Teddy asked.

Might as well, I said. *There's nothing here for us.*

Chapter 17

In an instant, we were back on the dock. Odd, I know, but where were we supposed to go?

What now? I asked Teddy. *I don't want to go home because my husband the murderer is there.*

Let's go to my apartment, Teddy said. *Maybe we can talk things through and see if we can come up with a plan.*

As we floated into his living room, I said, *Nice place. Love your sectional.*

Thanks?

And you're really neat. You don't always expect that from a bachelor.

I aim to please. He laughed.

I floated into the kitchen where there was a large dog bowl and water bowl. *Tell me about Buck.*

His face reflected the loss he felt for his best furry friend.

What was he like?

Teddy gazed intently at his dog's bowls before he responded. *He was a rescue. A three-legged German shepherd. I've had him for seven years and he was four when I found him. He's what I'll miss most, I think.*

I looked away when I saw the pain in his eyes. I wanted to let him feel what he was feeling without having to talk about it.

When he grinned at the memories and shook his head, I knew the moment had passed.

How did he lose his leg?

He was attached to a K9 unit. The cops were chasing a bad guy with a gun. He shot at the cops and got Buck instead. When his leg couldn't be saved, he was surrendered to a shelter for service dogs. I was visiting the shelter looking for a dog and our eyes met. I knew immediately we had a connection. Best dog I've ever had.

You're a good person, Teddy.

He sank onto the sectional sofa, and I floated down beside him and took his hand. *We both left a lot behind*, I said.

Yeah. So . . . He slipped an arm around me. *What do we remember?*

I gave a sad laugh. *I think the last thing I remember is having lunch with Kiki the day before I died. Kiki's my best friend.*

Did you talk about anything meaningful?

Not really. We'd spent the morning shopping and grabbed a quick bite at the mall before we headed home. And then . . . that's all until I woke up dead. Weird, huh?

It's all weird, Teddy said.

At least you remember everything.

He looked away from me. *Not everything.*

But you remember being killed, and you remember seeing a person taking photos from the dock.

I may have embellished that, he said, a sheepish grin on his face. *I remember seeing that person, but it could have been before I went down to the boat. Or maybe they were taking pictures. It's all sort of foggy.*

We don't have a ton to go on, do we? I asked. *Looks like we're in the same boat. No pun intended.*

I got up and started pacing back and forth across the living room. *We got basically nothing from going to Lily Dale. I'd hoped the mediums would be more help than that.*

So, what do we do now? he asked. *I'm stumped.*

I tapped my lips with my index finger. *There was one thing both mediums told us.*

That got his attention. *What was that?*

That maybe we should find a good hypnotist.

He frowned. *Sure, because ghost hypnotists are so easy to find. Let's Google them.*

I don't think we'd find one that way, but we have Roz.

Who's Roz?

You met her . . . saw her . . . at my funeral.

The one who can see you. He brightened. *She's a hypnotist?*

Not yet, but she can learn. Kiki can help, too.

Chapter 18

We arrived at Roz's shop at ten the next morning. Our sudden appearance caused Roz to juggle her coffee mug sending the hot liquid flying up and out of the cup. And all over the front of the colorful gypsy-inspired outfit she was sporting today.

Oops, I said, by way of apology. *I'd be happy to clean that up. You know, if I could.*

She was busy shaking her head and muttering about stupid ghosts as she grabbed a handful of paper towels from the bathroom. She glared at me as she dabbed at the front of her purple-and-red peasant blouse and mopped up the wet floor of her reading room.

"Your BFF has been calling me to see if I heard from you," she called over her shoulder as she gingerly carried the dripping paper towels over to a wastebasket.

Can you call her and tell her I'm here? She could come join us if she wanted to.

"Sure. I'll jump right on it," Roz snarked.

You're in a mood today, I pointed out.

"I haven't had my coffee yet." She waved a hand down her front to indicate the wet garment. "Maybe you could wait next time until I set it down."

I'm really sorry. It's just . . . we need your help.

"We?"

Teddy's here. You can't tell he's here? I indicated Teddy beside me.

Roz rubbed her chin with her thumb and forefinger as she scrutinized the spot I'd indicated. "I see something. Like a disturbance in the force. Hey, you," she addressed Teddy, "can you concentrate on your aura or something to make yourself less invisible?"

Teddy looked at me questioningly.

Maybe if you hold your breath and squeeze your eyes shut . . .

Very funny, he said. But he closed his eyes and held his breath. When he opened one eye, he asked, *Can you see me now?*

Roz didn't respond.

I really don't know what to do, he said.

Concentrate on being present, I suggested. *I concentrated on those tarot cards when we were at Susie's, and I could move them.*

Concentrate on what?

Concentrate on wanting to let Roz see you?

"I'm starting to see an outline," Roz said. "He's not as solid as you are, Laurel, but maybe we're getting somewhere."

I could see the effort Teddy was making in his eyes, his gaze hard and looking inward.

I did my best, he said.

"I heard that," Roz said, and both our heads spun toward her.

Yay, I said. *It's so much easier if I don't have to translate.*

"Tell me about it," Roz said with a head shake. "So now what?"

Can you call Kiki and see if she can come over? I want to talk to both of you.

Roz shrugged. "Sure. No problem." She reached into a pocket in her flowing red skirt and pulled out her cell. After a quick conversation, she said, "Kiki will be here in twenty minutes. Now, while we wait, do you mind if I get myself another cup of coffee?"

It's liberating in a way when someone can see you, isn't it? Teddy asked.

It definitely makes things easier. And we need all the help we can get.

We stayed out of Roz's hair for a while to let her drink her coffee in peace. Teddy and I hung out and I showed him around, pointing out the Lily Dale book that had prompted our big trip.

Kiki breezed in, wearing tight black jeans and a really cute crop top, paired with stacked sandals. What? I could still appreciate a good outfit when I saw it.

"Is she still here?" Kiki asked. Kiki seemed much more sanguine, or maybe I should say unfazed, at interacting with a ghost. She was more her self-possessed self as opposed to the hyper, tiny-bit-scared Kiki from when she'd first been presented with the information that her best friend was now a ghost.

"Yeah," Roz said, waving toward the area where Teddy and I were standing.

Kiki looked in our general direction and spoke to the air. "Where have you been? What have you been doing?"

"She's here with her boyfriend, Teddy," Roz offered.

"She has a boyfriend?" Kiki looked perplexed.

He's not my boyfriend. *We're just friends. Fellow travelers through the mist.*

"Now who's being poetic?" Roz deadpanned.

"What did she say?" Kiki asked.

"She's in denial." Roz took a sip from her cup. "Coffee or tea?"

"I'd love some tea," Kiki said.

When Kiki was done fixing her cup of tea at the sideboard, she returned to Roz's round reading table. When they were seated and after they'd had a few sips of their beverages, I cleared my throat.

We need your help, I said.

"I figured as much," Roz said as Kiki looked on.

Lily Dale was a bust, I said, *pretty much. I mean, we talked to a medium and a psychic and unfortunately neither of them could do anything for us.*

But . . . I held up a finger. They suggested something that we want to try. I want you to hypnotize us.

Roz choked on her coffee, only barely avoiding spitting it out, thankfully, because it would have probably sprayed all over Kiki.

"What is it?" Kiki asked. "What just happened?

"The lovebirds took a short vacation to New York looking for mediums. Apparently, I wasn't good enough for them." She gave me the side-eye. "Anyway, the mediums turned out to be a big zero and now she wants us to . . . get this . . . hypnotize them!"

Kiki's eyes grew wide. "Hypnotize a ghost?"

"Two ghosts."

"I wish I could see them," Kiki said, glancing around the room.

Watch this, I said, and moved her teacup to the middle of the table, careful not to slosh anything out of it.

Kiki shrieked. "Was that her?"

"Yep. Looks like she's picked up a few tricks."

"That's so cool!" Kiki said, a wide grin on her face.

It made me smile.

Roz, do you think you could pull up a couple of chairs for us?

She frowned. "What do you need a chair for?"

Well, I don't want to talk down at you. If we have chairs, we'll all be on the same level.

"I'll have to get them out of the garage," she said. "Only two chairs came with this table."

She stood and nodded at Kiki. "Want to come help me?"

"Sure," Kiki said as she joined Roz. "Why did she say they want chairs?"

"I guess they want to feel like they're equal to us." She waved her hand dismissively. "Whatever."

In a couple of minutes Roz and Kiki returned with folding chairs and set one up on each side of the table.

"Okay. Tell us what you need," Roz said once we were all settled back down. "But I'm not promising anything."

I know. And I don't know if it will work or not, but we have to do something, or we'll be stuck here for eternity if we can't figure out what we need to know to cross over.

"But hypnotism?" Roz asked, quirking an eyebrow.

Don't hypnotists regress people all the time? I asked. *If you could help us to relive that time, maybe the answer will be there for us.*

"What's she saying?" Kiki asked. "I really wish I could see her."

"Your friend thinks hypnotizing them will help them solve the mystery of why they're stuck here."

"I don't know anything about hypnosis," Kiki said. "Do you?"

"Nope. I must have been absent the day that subject came up in class."

You can do it. I know you can. I need you to try to hypnotize me, I said.

"Now? Are you out of your mind?" Roz held up her hand as if to call a halt. "I can't hypnotize a ghost. I don't know how."

Not if you don't try, you can't.

"Come on. That's ridiculous."

You could at least try. Until we can remember what really happened to Teddy, neither of us can cross over. You have to help us.

Roz closed her eyes, shaking her head. "What am I supposed to do?"

Kiki watched Roz, trying to figure out what was happening.

I don't know. Say "You're getting sleepier and sleepier" or something. Like in the movies.

"Fine," Roz said. "Sit down."

At Roz's suggestion, I switched seats with Kiki so that I sat across the reading table from her. Roz put her hands on the table and I did the same. She leaned forward and I followed suit.

"Look into my eyes," she said, focusing her eyes on my eyes.

I focused right back, trying not to blink. We sat like that in silence for several minutes before a skeptical look crossed my face. *I don't think this is working. Maybe you need to say more words.*

Teddy looked on, curious about the process. *Should it be dark in here or something?* he asked.

Roz pulled the blinds closed, which made the interior of her reading room dim, then sat down again.

Say something about relaxing, I said to be helpful.

"What's—" Kiki started.

"Shush!" Roz snapped.

Roz rolled her shoulders, put her hands on the table, leaned toward me and intensified her stare.

"Relax your body, clear your mind as you listen to my voice. You're getting sleepy. As I talk, you're getting sleepier." She stopped and watched me. "Feeling anything?"

I shook my head. *Nothing. There must be more to it than that.*

"That's all I know about hypnotism," she said. "Sorry."

I get it, I said. *I know you're not a practicing hypnotist, obviously, but maybe you could Google how to do it. I'm sure there are YouTube videos of people hypnotizing other people.*

"Maybe Kiki can research it. I do have a job, you know."

"Laurel, can't you let me see you?" Kiki begged, as her eyes tried to pinpoint my location on the chair I was sitting in.

"Your boyfriend concentrated really hard and now I can see him," Roz said. "Why don't you try that for Kiki? That way I don't have to be the interpreter." She put a hand on Kiki's arm. "Not that I mind."

Sure. You don't mind helping her, but I'm a pain in the ass?

"You said it, I didn't," Roz smirked.

"Psst," Kiki said to Roz behind her hand. "What's her boyfriend's name?"

He's not my boyfriend! I said. I mean, kissing someone doesn't automatically make them your boyfriend, does it?

"She *claims* he's not her boyfriend," Roz said, making finger quotes. "But his name is Teddy."

"Is he cute?" A typical Kiki question.

"I can barely see his outline. Ask your friend."

Kiki looked expectantly toward my chair. I cringed as Teddy waited for my answer, a grin on his face.

He's a total hottie, I said, and flashed a grin back at Teddy.

"He's *adorable*," Roz translated with rolling eyes.

"Great! I can't wait to go find out how to hypnotize them," Kiki said and stood. "Laurel, can you work on making me see you?"

I scratched my head, not sure how to do that, but nodded.

"She's gonna try," Roz said.

Chapter 19

I'm a hottie, huh? Teddy wiggled his eyebrows. He stood aside and waved me into his apartment.

You kind of are, I said, with an embarrassed laugh. *What about me?*

You are drop-dead gorgeous . . . pardon the pun.

I laughed and leaned in for a kiss. Which he was happy to provide.

Do you think you'll be able to let your friend see you? he asked.

I don't have a clue how, although Roz was right. When you concentrated hard enough, she was able to see you. Of course, she's a medium, so there's that.

True. Do you think you can show me how to move things? It was impressive to see you do that.

I tapped a finger on my lips. Let's see. The first time at Carol the medium's, I was angry and just flung my arm out and those tarot cards went flying. Nothing really jumps out at me. How I made things move, I mean.

Teddy and I sat side by side on his couch. I glanced around the room, my gaze ending up on the remote control sitting on the coffee table in front of us.

I'll tell you everything I know . . . which isn't much . . . and I think we should both work on it. Practice.

Teddy nodded.

Look at the remote and push your energy toward it, I said. After a moment when nothing happened, I said, *Are you trying?*

Of course I'm trying. It's just not working. Did it work the first time you tried it?

I didn't try. *The first time was at Carol's, and I was really mad that she wouldn't acknowledge us. So, I must have thrown my energy without even thinking about it. The way you'd throw a glass at a fireplace if you were mad enough.*

Teddy laughed. *I've never been mad enough to throw a glass at a fireplace. You?*

Oh, shut up, I said. *Try to work up some anger and channel it toward the remote.*

He rolled his eyes, then closed them. And nothing happened. *I don't think that's the key,* he said.

It has to be. Maybe you're not emotional enough, mad enough. I stared at the remote for a moment and then looked at Teddy. *Try this. Hold your breath and try to blow it out. Pretend like you're blowing with all your might and blocking it with all your might. Maybe the energy will build to the bursting point.*

He shrugged. *Okay.* He focused his attention on the remote, and I could see the intensity in his gaze and the way his cheeks puffed out as he pretended to hold his breath. I also saw when he blew out his pretend breath and rubbed his hand through his hair dejectedly. *Nope. Nothing.*

This had to be the way. I was sure of it. Well, maybe not sure of it . . .

Do it again, I said.

Why?

Just do it. And if it doesn't work, do it again. I think since you're not manifesting a strong emotion you have to practice honing your focus. So, try again.

After ten tries, Teddy was ready to cry uncle. But I was totally into proving my theory by this point and couldn't let him stop. I wasn't sure, however, how far I could push him. New relationship and all.

Look. Just try three more times. If nothing happens, we'll think of something else.

He gave a weary sigh and stared daggers at the remote, his cheeks tight with his blocked breaths. Nothing. He made a low growl and squeezed his eyes shut for a second, then refocused on the remote. And noth—

Just as we both were giving up, the remote slid across the coffee table. Only a couple of inches, but that wasn't the point.

I jumped up. *You did it, Teddy!* Then I hopped around like a kid on her first visit to Disneyland.

He had a look of awe on his face. He reached out to touch the remote. Of course, his fingers went right through it. But he turned and smiled at me. *I did, didn't I?*

I grabbed him and twirled him around, and then we were kissing. It felt so right, but after a moment we pulled apart sheepishly, not looking at each other.

So, um, he managed, *what's next?*

I couldn't help myself. *This is so weird. We're ghosts and we're kissing. Are we even allowed to do that?*

You know as much about it as I do. Nobody gave us a rule book.

I know, but it's just not how I pictured ghosts acting, although there was a really old movie, from the thirties maybe, where George Kerby and his wife, Marion, were in a car accident and then they were able to be a ghost couple who haunted their old friend, Cosmo Topper. It was a comedy, though.

He tilted his head at me. *I'm not sure I pictured being a ghost at all, but there's no HR department standing over us telling us what we can and can't do. I don't know about you but having you here . . . it makes things better.*

It makes things better for me, too. I can't imagine going through this alone. I sat back down on the couch and rubbed my hands together.

What's next is, we practice this and keep practicing until we don't have to think about it, I said.

Teddy shot me a comic glare and turned his attention to the remote. It didn't move right away, but after a couple of tries it slid toward me.

It took me a couple of tries to slide it back toward him. Maybe I was distracted by that kiss . . .

Hours later, at least it seemed like hours, but who knows how ghost time works, we looked at each other with a sense of accomplishment. After the remote, we'd pulled books out of the bookcase (a standard haunting move), opened and closed kitchen cabinet doors, and knocked over a knickknack or two. Teddy even managed to float his softball trophy through the air.

You're a marvel, Teddy said. *Look what we can do because of you.*

Oh, thank you, I said with mock modesty. *I'm feeling pretty good about myself right about now.*

I floated back to the couch. *Now I need to figure out how I can make myself visible to Kiki.*

I think that must be a focus thing, too. Maybe you have to hold your breath really hard and puff out your cheeks—

Very funny. But you might be right. The only way to know is to go over to Kiki's and try it out. Come on. I grabbed his hand and wished us to Kiki's.

Chapter 20

We found Kiki hunkered down in front of her laptop, bless her heart. We watched over her shoulder for a few minutes as she was researching hypnotism. I took a deep breath and tapped her on the shoulder. She about shot out of her chair, looking around wildly.

Now I felt bad that I scared her.

I glanced at Teddy then closed my eyes and concentrated on giving my ghost self substance in the real world. When I opened them, Kiki was staring at me with big eyes and an open mouth.

"Laurel?"

She had that fight-or-flight look on her face, and I reached out toward her. *Kiki, don't be scared. It's me.*

She put a hand over her mouth, her big eyes still visibly gaping at me.

You said you wanted to see me. I can disappear again if you want me to.

She shrank back into her desk chair, never taking her eyes off me. I could see the fear was still there.

I promise I won't hurt you. I've been practicing and I wanted to see if I could make you see me. I waved toward the laptop. *And I wanted to see if you figured out how to hypnotize us.*

"Um, no," she stammered, then cleared her throat. "There are some procedures we can try. Of course, none of them are directed toward ghosts." She was warming to her topic. "Look here." She swung toward her desk and pulled the laptop closer. "This website mentions some tools we can use, like a candle and a crystal. The crystal should be on a chain so we can swing it back and forth in front of your eyes while you concentrate on it."

I wanted to hug her. My best friend was back. Not that she was the one who went away, but you know what I mean.

"Where's your boyfriend?" Kiki asked. "Is he here too?"

Teddy, you try it now and see if you can make yourself visible.

"Yes, because I'm dying to see what you look like," Kiki said, then made an embarrassed cough. "I mean, not *dying* but just—"

It's okay, Kiki, I said. *We get it. We're not offended.*

Teddy closed his eyes and concentrated.

See anything yet? I asked Kiki.

"Not yet. Do you think it's going to work?" She looked in the direction I had been speaking, not sure where Teddy might actually be. "Where is he?"

I stood right next to Teddy and pointed, leaning over and planting a kiss on his cheek.

"Ah," she said and stared at the empty air at my side. I could feel both of their focused attention on the task.

"Wait! I think I see something," she said. I could see Teddy tighten his jaw and try a little harder.

She jumped up and clapped her hands. "He's here!"

I laughed. *Kiki, this is Teddy. Teddy, meet Kiki.*

She giggled. "He's really cute."

Thanks, I said. *But he's not really my boyfriend. I mean, he kind of is, but we're ghosts so I don't know how it works.*

I glanced at Teddy. He hadn't spoken since I'd introduced them. I could see that he was afraid if he broke his concentration by speaking that he'd disappear. I bumped him with my hip and smiled at him.

I turned back toward the laptop. *Did you learn how to use that stuff? The crystals and candle. Can we try it now?*

"I want Roz to be there," Kiki said. "She's more into this woo woo stuff than I am. She'll probably know the best way to make it work."

Can you call her and see when we can do it? Not that I'm anxious or anything.

"I'll call her, but can we do it tomorrow? Mike's taking me out tonight."

Speaking of Mike, I said, *does he know about all of this?*

"I've told him, but I don't think he believes me. Or I think he believes me but he thinks there must be some other explanation than ghosts."

I'm not surprised. It's hard to believe what you can't see, I said.

"I'll meet you at Roz's around noon tomorrow. I'll make notes about what I can find on hypnosis. I have a good feeling about this. We're going to get your memory back."

• • •

We stopped at Roz's after leaving Kiki's to let her know the plan for tomorrow. I pointed out that we picked lunchtime so it wouldn't interfere with any client meetings.

After that, Teddy and I spent the rest of the day practicing our concentration. I couldn't help thinking that concentration might be important in hypnosis.

Not that ghosts get tired or anything, but we were mentally exhausted after spending hours moving things around in his apartment, and sank down next to each other on his couch.

I felt closer to this man than I'd ever felt to anyone. Maybe it was because I saw only his spirit, like he saw mine, not cluttered with the trappings of subterfuge, or the games people play, only the goodness in his heart. How did I get so lucky?

He was looking at me in a way that told me he was as in awe of me as I was of him. He leaned in and with his ghost hand brushed my ghost hair behind my ear, then kissed me. I closed my eyes and sighed, letting the ghost kiss carry me away. It felt real, even though *we* weren't real.

Do ghosts have sex? That would be weird, wouldn't it?

The thought caused me to pull back and look at him. His eyes held the intensity of his desire and he gently laid me back on the couch.

I heard him moan as our kisses deepened and I became aware that something extraordinary was happening. He lifted his lips from mine and pulled away, sitting up and then standing, his hand holding mine and pulling me to my feet. I watched, astounded, as his feet, then his legs, dissolved into mist that moved up his body. Looking down, I was dissolving into my own mist. The mist of his being and the mist of mine intertwined and spiraled around each other until we were indistinct from one another. We had no bodies, no heads, no faces, nothing but a burning light inside of each of us, a light that didn't hurt, but the warmth of our lights wrapped us together until we were one amazing force experiencing a sensation that no living person had ever felt. And never would.

We were bound now, as one, until the mist dissipated, and we found ourselves once again sitting side by side on Teddy's couch. We felt no need to speak of the incredible bonding. He wasn't a man, and I wasn't a woman. We were spirits. I looked at him in wonder.

This is what a soul mate is.

$$Chapter\ 21$$

We arrived at Roz's after Kiki, and my friend smiled and waved when she saw us appear in the parlor. I'm not sure Roz ever smiled. Not that I blamed her, as I had invaded her orderly life.

"When did this happen?" Roz asked Kiki, indicating me and Teddy.

Kiki's face lit up. "They dropped in on me last night and they kept trying different things, and finally it worked!"

"That must have taken some energy," Roz said. "Can you do anything else?"

We've been practicing our concentration, I said. *We can move things, too.* I glanced at Roz. *Like Kiki's teacup.*

"That was so cool," Kiki said.

"It certainly was," Roz grudgingly acknowledged. "We should get started, though."

Kiki launched into what she'd learned about hypnosis, and Roz had done her own Googling and had notes from her research.

From a tote bag, Kiki removed a candle and a teardrop crystal suspended from a chain. I'm sure it had been meant as a necklace and not as a tool.

She glanced around Roz's parlor and frowned when she didn't find a recliner or comfortable chair for her "patients." I'm sure that's what the instructions probably said was needed.

"I don't know if this will work if you can't relax," she said, tapping her lips with a finger in consternation.

I don't think it will be a problem, I said. *One surface is like another to a spirit. Roz's reading room setup is fine.*

Kiki picked up her tools and set them on the round table. She looked anxious.

"Why don't you let me do this?" Roz asked her. "I'm used to making my customers feel at ease."

Roz removed the potted plant from a tall plant stand in a corner of the room. She swiped a saucer from her sideboard and set the candle on it. Then she moved the plant stand next to her reading table and lit the candle. Roz motioned for me to take a seat, then told Kiki to turn out the light. Two windows in the room filtered light through thin venetian blinds, but the room was mostly dim.

"Laurel, you need to relax. I'll help you, but perhaps you could take some deep breaths."

I don't actually breathe, I said.

"Pretend then. Just humor me."

I made the motions of breathing deeply.

She held up the crystal pendant and swung it slowly back and forth. The flame from the candle reflected in the facets of the crystal necklace and I allowed my eyes to follow its swings.

"Put your hands in your lap and relax."

I followed her instructions, my eyes never leaving the swinging crystal, and I felt calmness cover me.

"Feel your muscles relax, starting with your toes, then your feet. The feeling of relaxation continues up your legs and continues further until your head drops forward."

Her voice had a mesmerizing quality to it and my ghost body did seem to be loosening and settling into the chair.

"Kiki! Stop hovering!"

"Sorry!"

I shook off the interruption of Roz being distracted by Kiki. I squeezed my eyes tight and fake-breathed in and out.

"Sorry about that, Laurel," Roz said. "Let's continue. You're standing at the top of a stairway. Breathe in and out and take a step down. We'll repeat the process for all ten steps. With each step, you'll feel yourself letting go of distractions and errant thoughts, and your body will relax more as you descend, and you'll become sleepier with each step. At the bottom, you will be deeply asleep. You will allow your subconscious to come forth with answers to your questions. When I count to three, you will awake, completely refreshed, and you will remember everything."

She counted off the steps and I concentrated on allowing myself to drift with her voice. I was getting so sleepy . . .

"1 . . . 2 . . . 3."

My head shot up and I felt a momentary confusion.

Did it work? I asked immediately.

"Do you remember?" Roz asked.

I think so.

"What do you remember?" Kiki asked.

Teddy watched me intently. *Do you know what happened? What you need to know?*

"I think if we repeat some of the steps that relaxed her, more memories will come," Roz said.

But do you know what happened? Teddy asked.

I had to think. I could feel the thoughts swirling in my head as I tried to make sense of the memories.

I saw you, Teddy. Before. We were in the parking lot at the marina, and I was walking toward our dock. You came up to me and pressed something into my hand. You told me your name and said if anything happened to you I should take it to the police. It was . . . it was . . . My face scrunched up as I looked down at the imaginary item in my hand. *It was a thumb drive. You gave me a thumb drive. What was on it?*

Kiki and Roz were hanging on my every word.

I'm a little fuzzy, too, he responded.

Roz, I said, *can you hypnotize Teddy? I think we both need to be in on what happened that night.*

She nodded, and I moved to let Teddy take the chair across from Roz, then she repeated the same process she'd used with me while Kiki and I watched silently.

Kiki snuck a quick smile at me. She reached for my hand but quickly realized she wouldn't be able to touch me, so she bobbed her head sheepishly and went back to watching Teddy and Roz.

It didn't work the first time, and Roz decided she was hungry, so she and Kiki left to grab sandwiches from the deli next door.

It's going to work, I said to Teddy. *We'll get to the bottom of this.*

He gave me a wry grin and patted my hand. He *could* touch me. I reached up and ruffled his hair.

Thanks, he said.

I wrapped him in a hug, for my benefit as well as his. I could feel his spirit mingle with mine, which made me feel warm and safe and loved as our misty souls floated and twirled in the air for a brief time before we settled back into our ghost forms. It was the pinnacle of being.

The little bell over the door tinkled and Roz and Kiki were back.

Roz rubbed her hands together. "Ready?" she asked, as she sat at her reading table and indicated the chair across from her.

She left him under for longer this time, and when she brought him out we all looked at him expectantly.

Did anything come back? I asked.

He didn't answer immediately, and I assumed he was waiting for his head to clear, but then he said, *I think it did.*

We need to sit down and flesh out the events and see if we can pin down the information we've been looking for, I said.

Kiki whipped an iPad out of her bag. "I'll take notes."

"So, what do you remember?" Roz asked.

Teddy scratched his head as we took our seats around the reading table. *I'd been following a lead for a long time, and things finally came together.*

"What kind of lead?" Kiki asked.

"Shhh, let him talk," Roz said.

I'm an investigator. Actually, an investigative journalist. I was working on a story about smuggling South American artifacts. It's a big, dangerous business.

"And Ethan was involved in it?" Kiki couldn't help asking.

He's one of the top guys running the Southern California operation.

What was on the thumb drive? I asked.

Proof. A copy of everything I'd turned up so far. Teddy's face changed to resignation. *I guess 'so far' is no longer correct, as I won't be adding anything more, but there's enough there to shut down the ring.*

"There's a ring?" Kiki asked, wide-eyed.

Yes. Organized crime is involved in a big way with the smuggling of artifacts all over the world. South America, the Middle East, Africa, Israel. Egypt. Even mummies are stolen to be sold to private collectors. It's an ugly world out there. I've been following a shipment of stolen pieces from Peru and Argentina coming up through Mexico. Ethan's shipping company is in a perfect position to move the goods.

"How did they get them?" Roz asked. "The smugglers, I mean."

There are a lot of poor people in those countries who can be tempted. Huecheros, people desperate to scratch out a living, steal from archeology sites, even churches and museums. There are lots of unexcavated sites as well that are looted by the huecheros. And more than one antiques dealer is willing to market stolen works from their shops.

He stopped talking. My head was swimming at this window into my husband's criminal activity.

"Interesting," Kiki said, "but how does this prove you were murdered?"

I looked at Teddy, wondering that myself.

I'm hoping you can answer that, he said to me.

"Laurel, do you remember anything else from that night?" Roz asked, clearly into the mystery.

There were memories swirling around in my head, I just needed to sort them out a little, so I stood and paced for a few moments. When I returned to my seat, I had an idea about what was so important for me to remember.

I didn't want to take the thumb drive from you.

I remember I had to practically beg you to help me, Teddy said.

Yeah. You told me a convoluted story about evidence against some criminal elements.

It was more than that, Teddy said. *I told you the meeting might go south and, if it did, I might not make it out alive. I'm pretty sure you didn't believe me.*

I didn't, at first. But I didn't get the feeling that you were lying, so I took the thumb drive and left.

"And that's it?" Kiki asked.

I rubbed my forehead and ran my hand down my face. *Not exactly. Teddy also told me which dock he was going to. It was ours. We often had cocktails on the boat. I was on my way to surprise Ethan. Teddy freaked when he found out I was Ethan's wife. I think he was sure I'd march down to the boat and tell Ethan what was going on. But Teddy asked me to trust him. He convinced me that it would be a very bad idea for me to be there. So, I left. For about two seconds. I waited until he was almost at the boat, then I snuck back. I couldn't believe what he told me about Ethan, but part of me wasn't absolutely certain it couldn't be true, so I wanted to watch to see what would happen. I stayed out of sight partially hidden by a large Ficus tree in the parking lot and . . . I don't know what possessed me, but I pulled my iPhone out of my purse and started to videotape what was happening and zoomed in as much as I could. When they tossed Teddy into the water, I gasped. I saw when Jeff*

Knight spotted me and pointed, and Ethan whirled toward me. I spun around and raced to my car and flew out of the parking lot like a bat out of hell. When I glanced in my rearview mirror, they hadn't yet crested the incline into the lot. I hoped they didn't recognize me. Apparently, I was wrong.

"Oh, my God, Laurel," Kiki said, concern in her eyes. "That must have been so frightening."

Believe me, it was.

"Then what did you do?" Roz asked.

I started to answer but realized I didn't know. *I don't remember.* My answer even shocked me. *Why don't I remember?*

"I'm not up to date on my hypnotism trivia," Roz said. A little snarky I thought. Not sure a jokey response was appropriate here. "Maybe your memory comes back in stages. Kiki and I can research it more. I have to believe if you remembered that much so clearly the rest is bound to come back. I just don't know how long it might take."

"Yeah," Kiki added. "Leave it to us, Laurel. We'll come up with the answer."

I saw the defeat in Teddy's eyes and couldn't help feeling like I'd let him down.

I stood and nodded to Teddy. *We should go. I'm sure Roz is right, and the rest will come back to me. In time.*

"I'm sorry, Laurel," Kiki said. She had tears in her eyes.

Oh, Kiki. It'll be all right. Don't cry. I can't even tell you how much I appreciate all that you and Roz have done for us. It's gonna work out. It just may take longer than we hoped.

Chapter 22

I was dejected. It seemed like the answer was *right there*, but it was still out of reach. And what are ghosts supposed to do when they feel hopeless? Despite the assurances I'd given Kiki and Roz, I wasn't optimistic. Why should I be?

Then I looked at Teddy, sitting on the dock (for some reason we often found ourselves back on the dock), head down, dangling his feet in the water. We couldn't both give up.

Tell me about your life, I said to him. *I mean, we're soul mates now and I want to know you completely.*

He looked up at me, I suppose measuring my intent, not sure he wanted to be jollied out of his black mood.

Not much to tell. I lived. I loved. I died.

That was informative, I said with a slight frown. *Who did you love?*

Jealous? He gave a forced laugh.

No, I'm not jealous. Is there some reason you don't want me to know about your love life?

He shook his head, looking down at the water. *There was just one love. Jade. I met her in college, and we lived together for four years.*

What happened to her?

Nothing happened to her. We just wanted different things. My career required traveling all over the world, looking into stolen goods and following up on leads. Jade wanted a more traditional life. She wanted kids and—

But you wanted kids.

Yeah, I did. But I always thought I had plenty of time.

Now we both looked at the water.

He glanced at me. *What about you? Were you in love with Ethan?*

I was . . . once. In the beginning of our relationship, I imagined he was my soul mate. It didn't turn out the way I expected. You know what's weird? Ethan loved visiting museums, especially ones with Latin American exhibits. We'd spend a whole day at the Getty, or the Huntington Library, or the Museum of Latin American Arts. We even got married at the Huntington Library. Coincidence? I think not. I teased him about being obsessed. Now I get the obsession. It was research for his side job.

Teddy gave a soft chuckle. *Hiding in plain sight.*

Who knew? I shook my head. *You know, Ethan and I were happy together for a long time. I was one of the fortunate ones. Until I wasn't.*

I guess there's that, Teddy said.

So, Jade, huh? I said. *Exotic name.*

She was an exotic woman. Long dark hair—

Like me? I flirted.

Yeah, he responded. *She was beautiful, like you.*

I gave him a big grin. *Did she break your heart?*

For a while there, I guess. But I got over it. Buck helped me get over her.

I didn't get over Ethan . . . because I didn't know I needed to.

He glanced at me again and shook his head. *Aren't we a pair of sad sacks?*

I'm not so sad anymore, I said, snuggling up under his arm, and he pulled me into an embrace.

Me, neither, he said into my hair.

<h1 style="text-align:center">Chapter 23</h1>

"Here's the deal," Kiki said, explaining what she'd learned about hypnotism from our experience the day before. "The most important thing is to let go of logic. If you let logic intrude, it will stand in the way of allowing your mind to go to the events you need to remember. We'll try to go a little deeper. I read that it's like watching a video. That sounds like what we're going for. And stress. Stress can interrupt the process, so just clear your mind. Can you do that?"

Bring it on, I said. I was pretty confident I could give myself over to the experience.

"By stress, I mean fear," Kiki continued. "You might be afraid it won't work, and that could hold you back."

Got it. Ready, Roz?

Roz had set up the candle and was holding the crystal pendant. "I'm ready. Sit down and we can start."

I watched as the crystal slowly swung back and forth. The light from the candle refracting off the facets of the crystal was mesmerizing. I suppose that's the whole point. I could hear Roz's voice as she attempted to lead me through a tangle of memories to land on the one that would hold the answer we were seeking. I could also feel my body relaxing and—

"1 . . . 2 . . . 3," Roz said.

I blinked rapidly and looked at the expectant faces waiting to hear what had happened. Especially Teddy's face, whose expression seemed to reflect that he was almost afraid to hope.

I smiled. *It worked. I think I remember everything.*

Cheers went up . . .

Everything seemed okay when Ethan got home that night. He asked if by any chance I'd come down to the marina, and I said no. He didn't bring it up again, so I thought he bought my denial, but obviously not. The next morning, I could hear him talking to someone on his cell while I was getting dressed. But he seemed fine when I said I had to go run some errands, and he walked with me to the stairs. Of course, that's when I felt the shove and ended up where I am now.

"Was that the big mystery you needed to remember in order to cross over?" Kiki asked.

Uh, no. What I needed to remember was where I stashed Teddy's thumb drive and my iPhone. I smiled. *I know where they are.*

"Don't keep us in suspense," Roz said, with a slight frown.

It's not as easy as you'd think coming up with a good hiding place, I said. *I stopped at the market and bought a box of watertight Ziploc bags, then drove to Aerie Park. I dropped the thumb drive and phone into one of the bags and zipped it shut. I tucked that bag into a second one, just in case. I didn't want to take a chance on the first bag leaking. I tied a string around it and dropped it in the pond at Aerie, where the lily pads are. The lily pads that are just down from the wooden bridge. I secured one end of the string under a rock sitting on the bank. Ethan wants my phone. He doesn't even know about the thumb drive.*

"What are we supposed to do?" Kiki asked.

You need to go get the evidence and take it to the police.

"Why would they believe us?" Roz said. "How would we even know where to look for this evidence?"

You can pretend you stumbled across it, I said, frustrated by the roadblock Roz tossed out there. *What's the big deal? And they won't doubt you when they see the evidence.*

"It's only a little after two," Kiki said. "Should we go now?"

Yes, yes, yes!

"I'll drive," Roz said. "Where is this Aerie Park?"

"It's in LA," Kiki and I said at the same time.

"Oh, great," Roz grumped. "At least it's not rush hour."

It's always rush hour in LA, I said. *Should we meet you there?*

"Why don't we all go together?" Kiki asked. "For moral support."

It was okay with me, so the four of us piled into Roz's car, Roz and Kiki in front and me and Teddy in the back. He glanced sideways at me and took my hand, which he held all the way to the park. It took about twenty minutes to get there. We found the parking lot surprisingly empty. Maybe because of the posted sign that said, "PARK CLOSED FOR MAINTENANCE," which we discovered when we marched up to the front entrance.

Oh my God! I yelled. I wanted to punch someone in the face. If it wasn't for the brick wall surrounding the park and the wrought iron gate, we might have tried to sneak in, but it would be just our luck to be discovered and escorted out of the park and have our package confiscated.

We can try again tomorrow, Teddy said.

But I didn't feel reasonable. I felt cheated and blocked and denied and stomped back to the car. *Let's just go*, I said.

It was a solemn drive back to Roz's. I was angry because no one was angry but me. Didn't they understand how important this was? I'd already been stuck on this plane for two weeks and I was ready to move on. Go for the gold!

"I'm sorry," Kiki said, when we'd filed back into the shop. "We can go back tomorrow. If it's convenient for Roz, how about around ten or eleven tomorrow morning?"

Roz nodded. "Either is fine."

"Then let's go with ten-thirty," Kiki said, waiting for me to nod my okay.

"Great," she said. "It's on. I'd suggest we all go to Starbucks or something, but you know . . . ghosts can't drink coffee." She looked at me questioningly. "Can you?"

I shook my head. *Nice thought, though.*

"Wait!" Kiki said. "We can still hang out even if you can't eat or drink. Want to come over and spend the evening with us?"

I'm sure Mike will be thrilled to not *see us,* I said.

I wouldn't mind doing something besides just floating around, Teddy said. *If you want to go, Laurel, then I want to go.*

I smiled at him as I considered Kiki's invitation. And decided Teddy was right.

What time should we pop in? I said, grinning at my ghost pun. *See what I did there?*

"I saw what you did. Glad you still have a sense of humor." Kiki looked at Roz. "You can come over, too, if you want."

"Oh, no. I—"

"Seriously. I'd love it if you came over, Roz. Since we're all in this together, we should get to know each other."

My best friend was such a good person. I loved that she invited Roz. Because by now Roz was my second-best friend.

"What the hell," Roz said. "Sure, I'll come over. Why not?"

Are you going to warn Mike about us? I asked, trying to picture his reaction.

"Mike will be fine with it. He knows what I've been up to with you and Roz."

"You mean he humors you, right?" Roz asked, with a twinkle in her eye.

"Laurel and Teddy will just have to convince him they're real," she said. "Trust me, guys. It will be fun!"

Chapter 24

I liked Mike for Kiki. He was a successful doctor, and he was kind and generous, and he adored Kiki. He spent two years in the Doctors Without Borders program and donated time to free clinics in disadvantaged neighborhoods. He treated Kiki like gold. And this was the happiest I'd seen her since she lost Arnie.

Teddy and I arrived the same time as Roz did. I got a kick out of the way Mike's jaw dropped open when he saw her. Roz had toned down her gypsy look a little. Instead of a long brightly colored skirt, she wore black jeans, but she still sported a brightly colored peasant blouse and bangle bracelets on each arm. And don't forget the red silk scarf in her hair. I think Roz was somewhere in her fifties. She could still pull off that look, but it wasn't something you see every day.

Mike covered it well, though, and offered a hand and a warm greeting. He didn't greet Teddy and me, but I guess that's to be expected.

"Laurel and Teddy are here, too," Kiki told Mike.

He looked like *what am I supposed to do with that information?* He had a blank expression on his face, with a touch of something, confusion maybe, mixed in.

"Okay," he said. "Can you point them out?"

"Yeah, they're standing next to Roz. Why don't we all go in the great room, and I'll get some drinks."

Mike glanced around, then shrugged as he followed Kiki.

"I've told Mike all about our big breakthrough," Kiki said.

"I have to admit that I'm intrigued, but forgive me if I'm a little skeptical," Mike said.

"So was I," Roz said. "Laurel's my first real ghost. Now I can see two of them."

"I was skeptical, too," Kiki said. "When Roz first called, I thought she was a crackpot, or maybe she was trying to blackmail me or something."

"Blackmail?" Roz said, narrowing her eyes at Kiki. "Whatever would give you that idea?"

"Well, you have to admit that I didn't really know you. Laurel and I made one visit to your shop for a reading and then out of the blue you call me? I was thinking, *what could she possibly want?* Sorry, Roz."

Roz laughed. "No problem." She looked at Mike. "If it was hard for me and Kiki to believe, I can only imagine what you thought."

He shook his head. "It was all really weird. When Kiki told me she needed to go find out if her friend Laurel was okay and that she needed me in case there was trouble, I scratched my head a bit. But when we got there and saw Laurel's body . . . I didn't even have to check for a pulse. It was obvious she was already gone." He looked around the room. "Sorry, Laurel. I hope I didn't offend you."

I'm not offended, I said. *I was already dead.*

"She said no problem," Kiki offered.

"It was obvious that Laurel's husband was acting oddly," Mike said. "He wanted to rush us out of the house, and don't forget he lied about calling 911."

He picked up his glass of Scotch and took a sip. "Then you started saying you didn't want to believe it," he said to Kiki.

"I didn't want to tell him the ghost part at first," Kiki said. "I mean, he's a doctor so I didn't think he'd believe me."

"Just because I'm a doctor doesn't mean I don't have an open mind," he said.

Kiki patted his arm. "I know, honey. But you can have an open mind and still not believe in ghosts."

"When did she tell you?" Roz asked.

"When we got home that afternoon after the . . . the . . . after Laurel was taken away. I thought Kiki was just sad about her friend, but she kept saying Roz was right. I asked what she was talking about and, at first, she wouldn't say, but after a glass of wine or two she told me about Roz and the ghost of Laurel. This was after she'd gone to Roz's, I guess to tell her and Laurel what had happened."

"Mike didn't really want me to go since I'd just had a big shock, but I knew you'd want to know."

"Laurel was on pins and needles until you got there," Roz said.

"Anyway, I sort of filled Mike in when I got back . . . having a glass of wine or two helped. I told Mike about Teddy later on and that you were trying to find something but didn't know what it was. He was pretty skeptical about the hypnosis thing, though."

"And now supposedly Laurel remembers hiding her iPhone and a thumb drive in a lily pond," Mike said. He took another sip of his Scotch and set the glass down on the coffee table. "And tomorrow you're going to go get it."

I glanced at Teddy and winked, then I slid Mike's glass a few inches and then moved it back. I got a big kick out of watching his eyes bulge out.

"What the f—?"

"Laurel just wanted to show you she's really here," Kiki said. "Do you believe me now?"

Mike gulped. "I . . . I didn't *not* believe you, but . . . " He tentatively picked up his glass for another sip. "I guess truth really *is* stranger than fiction."

"Do you want to see them?" Kiki asked Mike. "Maybe they could, you know, make themselves visible."

"It's a trip," Roz said with a grin. Maybe a throwback to her hippy days.

If she had hippy days. I don't know her that well.

Mike didn't answer right away. I think he might have been a tiny bit overwhelmed after my demonstration. The color had drained out of his face. I imagine he wasn't sure how far down the rabbit hole he wanted to go.

"Can you?" Kiki asked me. "Make yourself visible?"

If it's okay with Mike, we can try.

"She said it's up to you," Kiki said to Mike.

"Oh, what the hell," he responded, picking up his glass and taking a big gulp. "I might need another Scotch for this, though."

Kiki smiled and carried his glass into the kitchen to refill it.

When she was back, she handed Mike his glass and raised her own. "Let's toast to Mike joining the Ghost Club."

"I'll drink to that," Roz said, clinking her wineglass against Kiki and Mike's glasses.

Tell him he has to relax. He should take some deep breaths, I said.

Kiki relayed my instructions. Mike looked a little fearful, but he took a deep breath.

"Maybe you should close your eyes," Kiki said. "It might help you to clear your mind."

Mike sat forward, forearms on his knees, hands clasped, and closed his eyes. Teddy and I held hands and focused our concentration on Mike.

"Is it working?" Kiki whispered. I had to work extra hard not to break my concentration. I gave a small shake of my head, and she took the hint.

I felt a slight change in the molecules in the room and Teddy and I stopped. *Open your eyes*," I said to Mike.

"Huh?" Mike said, then slowly opened his eyes. And jumped a foot off the sofa when he saw me and Teddy sitting beside Roz. He immediately grabbed for his Scotch.

Hi, Mike, I greeted him with a wiggle of my fingers. *This is Teddy.*

Hey, Teddy said.

Mike gulped his Scotch. "This is so weird."

I beg your pardon. I feigned insult. Then laughed. *You think this is weird? Try being a ghost for a while.*

Mike ran a hand through his hair and leaned forward, studying me. He cleared his throat. "You don't have any blood on you."

I was surprised at his comment, then understood. *I'm lucky that way. I get to wear the nice clothes I died in, and my fingernail which broke off in the fall is right back on my finger.* I waved my complete hand at him so he could see. *Can you imagine how creepy it would be if I did have blood all over the back of my head and down the back of my dress?*

"What about you, Teddy?" Mike asked. "What happened to you?"

Teddy glanced at me for a moment, then looked down at his hands. *Laurel's husband drowned me.*

"Huh. You aren't all wet."

"Mike, that's kind of inappropriate, don't you think?" Kiki said, while Roz took in all the questions and answers.

"Sorry," Mike said, bobbing his head. "It's the doctor in me, I guess. I analyze things. I hope I didn't offend you. Either of you."

No offense taken, man, Teddy said, offering a small smile.

"Wow. This is a fun party!" Roz said, lifting her glass in a faux toast. "Maybe we should start over. Kiki, you thought it would be nice for all of us to get to know each other. We've all been under a lot of pressure since this started, so why don't we just have a couple of drinks and relax?"

"That's a great idea. Laurel and Teddy, I hope Mike didn't put you off by his directness, and, Mike, I'm sorry this is so weird, but I'm really glad you can see everyone now. Okay, everyone, take a deep breath. And then take a big gulp."

We all laughed.

Mike cleared his throat again. "It's a pleasure to . . . see . . . you," he said to Teddy and me, and laughed nervously.

Kiki kissed him on the cheek. "Thanks, hon."

Mike turned and kissed her back. "I have to apologize for ever doubting you, Kiki. I mean, I knew you believed what you were saying, but it was a little too farfetched for me."

He picked up his Scotch glass and took a sip. When he set the glass down, he seemed ready to get down to business. "What's your plan?" he asked.

Kiki and Roz both started to respond, then I said, *I told them where to find the evidence—*

"Evidence of what, exactly?" Mike asked.

"Of murder," Kiki said.

"And smuggling of artifacts," Roz added.

"Hmm. Okay, go on," Mike said.

We tried to go retrieve the items, which I hid at Aerie Park, but the park was closed for maintenance. Can you imagine the bad timing?

"So, we're going back tomorrow," Kiki added.

"Need any help?"

"Not unless something goes wrong," Roz said. "It should be easy to pull the Ziploc out of the pond. Then we just have to give the evidence to the cops."

"Easy peasy," Kiki added.

"You just jinxed us!" Roz said, grasping her throat. "Quick! Knock on wood."

We all looked at Roz. Who knew she was superstitious?

"Geez!" Kiki said, knocking on the mahogany end table.

"You can't be too careful with this stuff," Roz said.

"We're safe now," Kiki said. "Wood knocking—check."

I, for one, am a tiny bit worried that something could go wrong. It seems too easy. I glanced at Teddy. And if it goes the way it's supposed to, we could be on our way to the Great Beyond by tomorrow night. I'm going to miss you guys.

"I hadn't thought of that," Kiki said, her wide eyes reflecting her alarm. "I'll miss you, too." She sat back and crossed her arms in a pout.

You'll at least know we're still here, I said, waving my arms, *in the ethereal sense. Even if you can't see us anymore, you know death isn't the end of the adventure.*

"Very poetic," Roz said. "Mind if I use it?"

Thank you. Feel free to quote me.

"I wish I had some ghost wine for you," Kiki said. "Or ghost beer in case Teddy doesn't like wine. So we could make a toast to our success."

"Not again!" Roz screeched. "Will you stop trying to jinx us?"

Kiki rapped on the end table again. "Good grief. Get a grip. See? I knocked on wood."

Maybe we should call it a night, I said. *We don't want to give Roz a heart attack if Kiki keeps trying to sabotage our mission. Besides, we don't want to overwhelm Mike with our presence.* I smiled at him. *Although you're taking it all very well.*

He laughed. "I'm feeling pretty honored. It's not everyone who gets to have drinks with a pair of ghosts. My fingers are crossed for your success tomorrow." He gave a sheepish grin. "I didn't jinx it, did I, Roz?"

"No. You're good."

This was nice. It was almost like still being alive. Almost.

Chapter 25

"Where is it?" Kiki shrieked, her face stark white in alarm. We were all standing on the bank of the pond, and the string I'd anchored to a rock was missing.

"Did the park workers find it and throw it away?"

First of all, I said, *they wouldn't have thrown it away. It was a top-of-the-line cell phone. Nobody would throw an eleven-hundred-dollar iPhone away. But who knows what they would have done with it?*

"We should find a maintenance worker to ask," Roz said. "Surely, they would remember finding our package. Spread out, everyone. We need to find a park guy."

"I wish Mike were here," Kiki said. "He'd know what to do."

"*We* know what to do," Roz snapped. "We can ask a question as well as a man could."

"Sorry," Kiki said. "I didn't mean it that way, exactly. I just meant that there would be more of us to cover the area, so we could find the guy quicker."

Roz sniffed. "Okay. No problem."

We all separated to search the park. There were trees and shrubs and flowers and bushes, and the terrain was rolling, so the search wouldn't be a snap.

I couldn't help feeling dejected. It was like the universe was working against us. If I'd just remembered a day earlier . . .

"What ifs" weren't helpful, and neither was feeling defeated. I refused to believe that the evidence was completely gone.

But I could see how down Teddy was. We'd both been counting on today being the day we'd be set free.

Teddy and I had the ability to float up and get an overview of the park, and our bird's eye view of our search area turned up no maintenance guy. Damn it.

I was angry. Angry at fate that had thrown us into this spectral situation and angry that fate seemed to be throwing up roadblocks.

Teddy and I sank down on the bank to wait for Kiki and Roz. Both looked hot and dejected when they rejoined us.

"Nothing," Kiki said. "You?"

"Me neither," Roz responded. They both looked at me.

I shook my head.

"You jinxed it!" Roz scowled at Kiki. "I *told* you."

"I did not! Besides, I knocked on wood to erase the jinx."

Kids, kids, I said. *This isn't helping.*

"What do we do now?" Roz asked.

I give up, I said. *What* do *we do now?*

I think we have to come back tomorrow, and if that doesn't work then the next day, Teddy said. *We have to talk to the maintenance crew.*

There really wasn't another option at this point. Kiki and Roz had checked some of the trash receptacles in case the park guy had tossed the bag. I hoped that wasn't what had happened, since the trash bins had been emptied before we got there. If our evidence was in one of them, we were totally out of luck.

"So, meet back here tomorrow?" Kiki asked.

Roz made a grouchy face but nodded. After goodbyes, both of them left.

Sorry, Teddy. It's all so unfair. I wandered over to the water. *It's my fault. It was a stupid hiding place. But I didn't want to keep it with me, because I didn't know what Ethan would do when he got home.*

Teddy gave a half-hearted chuckle. *If you'd taken it home with you, Ethan would have it now. Your plan was kind of ingenious, actually. The fault was in the timing, which you couldn't have known about.*

I sank down on the bank at the water's edge, and Teddy joined me. Neither of us felt anything but let down. He put his arm around me, and I felt safe and warm and . . . loved.

There was no way to describe our crushing disappointment. We were adrift here on this plane. We weren't supposed to be here, but we couldn't leave. All our hopes were tied up in finding the evidence that would prove our deaths weren't accidental, a result that would set us free to go into the light. It was like a death, almost, the way the answer was right in our grasp and the end of our entrapment here on earth was close enough to touch, then it was snatched away, leaving us neither here nor there.

We hadn't moved by the time Kiki arrived the next morning, because . . . why? She sat on the bench just up from the water and offered an optimistic appraisal of our chances for finding the "prize" by the time we left today. It was a sweet attempt to raise our spirits, no pun intended.

When Roz joined us, we formulated a plan of attack for the day which included another sweep of the park. Which, unfortunately, didn't turn up any maintenance men.

Roz surprised Kiki by hauling a cooler out of her car which contained sandwiches and bottled water. And chocolate chip cookies. Boy, do I miss cookies.

"You guys should have seen Mike after you left," Kiki said between bites. "He was so taken aback by the fact that ghosts actually exist. He's a doctor. He sees death on a regular basis, and he'd never even considered that death wasn't the end of the line. He feels honored that you opened his eyes."

I'm glad he's onboard. I like Mike, and I trust Mike, I said. *Maybe seeing us will give him extra insight into how he deals with his patients. Maybe he can reassure them in a way he wouldn't have been able to before.*

Kiki's head whipped around. "Is that—?"

A maintenance truck came into view, driven by a—wait for it—maintenance man.

When he pulled to a stop, Roz and Kiki immediately began grilling him. It took a minute for him to realize what they were talking about, then he held up a hand. "So, you lost something, and you think I might have found it?"

"Exactly," Kiki said. "Did you find anything . . . unusual?"

"Unusual, huh?" The maintenance man's nametag read Kevin. "Can you describe what you're looking for?"

Both Roz and Kiki looked at me for an answer. Before I could respond, the maintenance guy said, "Sorry. I didn't find anything."

I noticed immediately when Kevin's eyes changed to shrewd. And I immediately didn't trust him.

Kevin and his maintenance truck drove away, leaving us even more dejected and confused.

There's something off about that guy, I said. *I think we should go see what he's up to.* Teddy and I followed the truck, staying with it until he parked in the maintenance yard.

Kevin climbed off the truck and fumbled in the pocket of his uniform for a pack of cigarettes, shook one out, and dug in another pocket for a lighter. He lit up and sauntered to the edge of the lot, then leaned against an old pickup while he smoked the cigarette. I could see the wheels turning in his head as he tried to figure out how he could take advantage of the situation.

After a minute, he dropped the cigarette butt and ground it out with the toe of his boot. Reaching into his back pocket, he pulled out a phone and quickly tapped in a number.

We waited as he held the phone to his ear, curious what he might be up to. Maybe nothing, but it couldn't hurt to make sure.

Glancing around the parking lot to confirm he was alone, Kevin thoughtfully hit the speaker button. "Hey, Kyle," he said when someone answered. "I think something just dropped into my lap. It could be a nice score."

"What's the deal?" Kyle asked.

"I ran into these two ladies in the park today. They lost something. One of them was real hoity-toity, if you know what I mean. She didn't look like no suburban housewife. I smell money."

"What about the other one?"

"She was like some reject from the Sixties. Bracelets all over her arms. I saw a Range Rover in the lot. I bet it's the rich lady's."

"So, what's the score?"

"I tell them I found their package and say it'll cost them to get it back."

"You think they'll pay?"

"If they want it back, they will."

"Do you have it?" Kyle asked.

"Nah. But they don't know that."

I glanced at Teddy. He shook his head in disgust. *Let's go*, he said, and we went back to join Kiki and Roz by the pond.

I had just finished filling them in on what we overheard when the maintenance truck came back into view.

Let's play along, I said. *I can't wait to hear what he comes up with.*

Kevin climbed out and sauntered over. "I think I may know where your package is," he said.

"Oh, great!" Kiki said, pretending to be excited. "Where?"

"Don't be in such a hurry," Kevin said.

"Why don't you tell us what you found?" Roz said.

"Were the things inside valuable?" Kevin asked.

"What?" Roz's bangles jingled as she put her hands on her hips and glared. "What difference does that make?"

"You tell me. I might want to find out what I'm giving up before I make a decision."

"Look. You either found something or you didn't. If you didn't, stop wasting our time," Kiki said, pretending to barely contain her anger.

"You're an impatient one, aren't you?" Kevin said, eying Kiki appraisingly.

"My friend lost something," Kiki sniped. "You have no right to blackmail her."

"That's not blackmail," Kevin said. "Besides, how do I know what I found is really your friend's."

"What do you mean?" Kiki asked.

Kevin shrugged.

"Well, then, what did you find?"

"I'm not saying. But whatever it was, if you want it back it's going to cost you."

"You're despicable!" Kiki stomped her foot. "I should report you."

"Go ahead, but, if you do, you'll never get your package back." He climbed back into the truck.

"We won't get it from you, anyway," Kiki said. "You can tell your friend, Kyle, that your *score* fell through."

Kevin's mouth dropped open, and he sputtered, "How ... how do you ... you couldn't have heard—"

"The jig's up, creep," Roz said. "You should get out of my face before we report you."

There were thunderclouds in Kevin's eyes as he glared lightning bolts at her. He stood huffing and puffing for a full minute trying to figure out what had just happened, as we looked on silently.

Kiki wiggled her fingers at him. "Ta ta."

The maintenance man stomped back to his truck and burned rubber out of there.

"That was fun," Roz said grimly. "Too bad it left us with no other options."

I want to search this area again, I said. *Maybe we missed something.*

It's possible, Teddy said. He crossed his arms and looked thoughtfully at the pond for a moment. *It could have fallen in the water.*

But it was anchored by the rock, I said.

Maybe if Kevin or somebody accidentally kicked the rock the string might have slipped loose. The bag would drag it down pretty quickly.

"What?" Kiki said, scrunching up her face at the thought of the slightly less than pristine pond. "We'll never find it if that's the case."

Not necessarily, Teddy said.

He and I both leaned over to look into the water. We couldn't see the bottom, but we could see small fish darting in and out among the lily pads. *If it is in there,* I said, *we need to get it out quickly before those fish manage to nibble their way through the Ziploc bag.*

"We need a stick or something," Roz said. "We don't know how deep the water is or if the bottom's flat." She glanced around. "Just our luck. Of *course* the maintenance guys would pick up a branch as soon as it fell off."

"Well, I might have a golf club in my car," Kiki said. "Mike and I play sometimes."

"Go get it then," Roz said.

"Geez. Give me a minute. I just thought of it."

Kids, kids, I teased them. *Do I have to separate you?*

It was my turn to be on the receiving end of one of Roz's withering looks.

Kiki was back with her putter within moments, but she had to pretend it was a cane while a family of four arrived to admire the view. The two kids knelt by the bank and stuck their hands in the water in a vain attempt to catch the little minnows darting away from grasping fingers.

Roz practically exploded from holding her tongue. I could almost see the frustration rising off her in waves. She had to content herself with staring at her clenched fists in her lap. Kiki pretended to be absorbed by her phone. Teddy and I were picturing all the mud the children were stirring up, which would make locating the Ziploc that much harder.

The family moved on after about ten minutes. Once they were out of sight, Kiki brandished her golf club in the direction of the pond, but hesitated.

"Let me," Roz said, taking the club. "You're too squeamish."

Kiki didn't protest, and Roz stuck the club in the water, which came up almost to the top of the handle. "Ooh, that's pretty deep," Kiki said.

She looked pleadingly at Roz. "Um, which one of us is going to go in?"

"Neither of us today," Roz said. "We're not dressed for it. We have to go change, get a rubber suit or something."

"Yeah," Kiki agreed. "A rubber suit." She started to smile, then said, "Wait. What?"

"Maybe we can rent a scuba outfit," Roz said as she poked around the bottom of the pond. She looked at me. "I don't suppose you two with your special abilities could go down there and see where it is so we don't have to spend all day searching."

I glanced at Teddy with raised eyebrows. *We could give it a try.*

"You'll look like a mermaid down there in that billowy dress," Kiki said. "I hope it doesn't ruin it."

This dress is indestructible, I said. *Remember, it's got to last for eternity.* I turned to Teddy. *Ready?*

"Let's do this, he said with a grin, then turned and slipped into the water. I followed close behind.

It was murky. The silt and mud hadn't settled from swirling children's hands. I swam, or whatever it is we do to move through the water below the surface, to Teddy and took his hand. We could barely see each other through the dimness, but he pulled me to him and kissed me. It was kind of nice but distracting. I wondered if Kiki and Roz could see us, since the water wasn't extremely deep.

We each got as close to the pond's bottom as we could and started covering the area. Because of the murk, we tried using our hands to feel along the bottom, although, since our hands would go through whatever was down there, that turned out to be a less than useful idea. Back to using our eyes. We were able to move through the lily pad stems instead of having to weave our way around them. A small blessing, but not one to be disparaged.

Teddy found it first. It had slid or floated away from the bank, about six feet out. He stood and pointed out the spot to Roz and Kiki.

"How do we mark it?" Kiki asked, I'm sure picturing herself submerged among the lilies, searching unsuccessfully.

You don't have to, Teddy said. *I'll stand on the spot so you can't miss it.*

He and I appeared again on the bank. I struck a model's pose for Kiki, to show her that my dress was still perfect.

"Can you guys come over to my house?" Kiki asked. "So, we can make plans. I'll ask Mike if he can join us."

Chapter 26

"Where do we get a rubber suit?" Kiki asked, her anxiety over the great lily pond caper etched on her face.

"How deep is the water?" Mike asked. He'd listened intently as Roz recounted our day's adventures.

"As deep as a golf club," Kiki said. "The putter."

"We thought a scuba shop—" Roz started.

"That may not be necessary," Mike said. "Do you know what waders are?"

"Um, no," Kiki said.

"For fishing, right?" Roz said.

"Right. I happen to have top-of-the-line waders. They come up to here." He indicated his chest.

"But we have to go into the water to get it," Kiki said. "When we bend over, all the water will get in."

Oh, Kiki. She's so practical.

"Hmm," Mike said, tapping a finger on his chin. "Wait a minute. I've got it!"

"What?" Kiki asked, brightening. "What have you got?"

"We need to get one of those things you use to get something off a high shelf. I'm sure Target has them."

I don't know, Teddy said. *I'm worried it might puncture the bag. If water gets in, the evidence might be unusable.*

"You can put it in rice," Kiki said. "I read that dries phones out."

"What about the thumb drive with all the evidence?" Roz asked, shooting her a skeptical glance.

"Look," Mike said. "If you're careful, that shouldn't be a problem. Slow and steady."

"I suppose I have to do it," Kiki said, showing a little fear. "Unless you—"

"I don't think so," Roz said. "You're younger and can afford to replace your wardrobe if you get any water in those waders."

You can do it, Kiki, I offered in a tone I hoped was encouraging. *It'll only take a couple of minutes and the waders will mostly protect you. Please, Kiki? We need you.*

Kiki made puppy dog eyes at Mike.

"Stop!" he said, making his two index fingers into a cross to ward off Kiki. "I don't have surgery tomorrow. I'll do it. Happy now?"

Kiki's smile lit up the room.

Thank you, I said. I took Teddy's hand and squeezed it. *It means a lot to us that you want to help.*

"It's my first ghost caper," he responded. "How could I say no?"

We were back bright and early the next morning, ready as soon as the park opened, hoping there would be fewer visitors than later in the day.

"How do we do this?" Mike asked. He stood on the bank of the pond. Teddy and I had carefully scouted the park to make sure no one was headed our way. But we needed to move fast.

I'll stand in the spot where the bag is, Teddy said. *You should be able to retrieve it easily. If you use that grabber thing you won't even need to hold your breath.*

By now, Mike had donned his waders and Teddy was standing in the pond to show the location. Kiki handed Mike the grabber. He contemplated it for a moment, then handed it back to her. "It's quicker if I just bend over and pick it up."

I made another quick perimeter search to make sure we weren't about to be surprised by unwelcome visitors, then gave Mike the all-clear. He waded out into the pond until he was standing near Teddy, and Teddy pointed to the X-marks-the-spot. Mike took a deep breath and ducked down into the water. He felt around the bottom for a few seconds then swooshed up clutching the soggy-looking Ziploc bag, string dangling down.

Kiki and Roz cheered and jumped up and down in excitement, until I told them to cool it so they didn't draw any attention. Within a minute, Mike had waded out and was clambering out of his waders. Kiki handed him a towel and he did his best to soak up the water, then draped the towel around his shoulders.

"Let's get out of here," he said, picking up his keys and phone and leading the way to the parking lot.

I joined Teddy in the pond. We held each other tight, basking in our joy at recovering the evidence.

"Are you coming?" Kiki called to us. "We're going back to my house."

We'll meet you there, I said.

I wanted some time alone with Teddy.

Chapter 27

Half an hour later, we all reconvened at Kiki's to make sure the phone and thumb drive were undamaged.

It would be the first time I would view, on video, Teddy's murder, and I wasn't sure I wanted to see it, but it was important and, I hoped, would be vivid enough for the police to be able to use it against Ethan and Jeff. I gave Kiki my password so she could unlock the phone and pull up the video, and we all sat silently as the video played.

Afterward, no one spoke for several moments.

"You're good," Mike said. "The detail in the video leaves nothing out. We saw both Jeff's and Ethan's faces when they turned to look toward you. And we see . . . I'm sorry, Teddy. We see Teddy's body in the water."

I feel like I just relived that, Teddy said. *It wasn't pleasant the first time.*

"That's an understatement," Roz said. "To quote Laurel, that Ethan is a rat bastard."

What about the thumb drive? I asked. *Can you get your laptop, Kiki?*

You won't find a smoking gun, Teddy said. *But someone familiar with the illegal South American artifact trade will know what to do with it.*

"Do we know anyone like that?" Kiki asked.

My friend, Link. We were working together on this, but he was in the background of the investigation. We wanted it that way, in case . . . you know . . . something happened to me. We didn't want the bad guys to go after him, too.

"He must be suspicious about what happened to you."

I'm sure he is. He's probably looking into it himself. He would have searched for evidence of what I might have found out. But he's careful, and I don't think he would have been discovered.

"So, what do we do next?" Mike asked. "I'm guessing we need to pass the phone and thumb drive on to someone."

Yes, I said. *We can give the thumb drive to Link and the phone to the police.*

"Won't they have questions about why this suddenly turned up?" Kiki asked.

"And how we got hold of it?" Roz added.

I've been thinking about that, I said. *Kiki, you can say I called you after I left the marina and told you what I'd seen and that I was afraid Ethan knew it was me.*

"Yeah, but why didn't I tell the police that after you died?" she asked.

"Um, you didn't want to get involved?" Roz said. "You didn't want your name in the news?"

"But she was my best friend. Of *course* I would want her death investigated."

Did the cops talk to you again, ask you any more questions? I asked.

"No, I didn't talk to them again."

Hmm, I said. *You have to say that you couldn't accuse Ethan of murder. It would be slander or something.*

"How did the evidence turn up?" Roz asked. "I mean, if Kiki had it all this time, why did she wait so long to turn it in?"

God. Why is this so difficult? I asked. *We worked so hard to find it and now we can't use it?*

"I wouldn't give up yet," Mike said. "This is just logistics, and we can figure it out."

Can you get the thumb drive to Link? Teddy asked.

"That will be the easy part, so, yeah," Mike said.

I think you should call and have him meet you someplace public, Teddy said. *I don't want anything to lead back to him.*

"I'm good with that. You want to give me his number?"

Teddy provided it and Mike dialed.

When Link didn't answer, Mike left a message saying that he was a friend of Teddy Rule's and needed to meet with him.

"Won't he be suspicious?" Roz asked. "If it's all this cloak and dagger, Link might suspect that you're one of the bad guys who somehow discovered the connection between Teddy and Link."

Yeah, Teddy said. *He might. See if he calls back. If not, we'll go there and somehow we'll persuade him.*

"What about the phone?" Roz asked.

"Maybe I could say I found it on my porch the morning you died. I had it in my purse when I went to your house, but after finding you dead, I forgot about it. It got lost in the bottom of my purse and I just discovered it."

Yeah, except everyone who knows you knows you switch purses regularly to go with your outfits.

"There is that," Kiki said.

But you could say that you couldn't bear to look at it at first. When you finally did, you watched the video and knew the police had to have it.

"That's brilliant!" Kiki said, clapping her hands.

What do you guys think? I asked the group.

"Sounds plausible to me," Mike said. "Kiki was distraught after seeing your body and moped around for days. We could say she called me as soon as she watched the video and I told her we had to get it to the police."

My brilliant friends, I said with a satisfied sigh.

I think you should wait on the police until you give Link the thumb drive and he has the evidence he needs, Teddy said. *We don't want to tip off Ethan and Jeff that anything's up. One way or another, we'll take them down.*

"So, we'll just keep the phone and thumb drive here until we hear from Link?" Kiki asked.

"Let me take them," Roz said. "There's a connection between you and Laurel. If Ethan started snooping around, we don't want there to be any possibility of his finding anything. He doesn't know me from Adam."

She's right, I said.

"I think so, too," Mike said.

He started to hand the Ziploc to Roz, but Kiki said, "Eww. That one's a little stinky from being in the water. Let me get a clean one."

"Thanks for thinking of that," Roz said with a laugh. "I appreciate it."

Let's meet back here in the morning, I said. *Maybe by then Link will have called.*

"Sounds good to me," Mike said. "We've all had quite a day."

Chapter 28

Later, sitting side by side on the dock with Teddy, I said, I've been thinking. Don't you think it's strange that no one broke into your apartment. Ethan and Jeff, I mean. Wouldn't they want to see if you had anything incriminating there?

I've thought about that, too. The only thing that occurred to me is that by ransacking my apartment it might rouse suspicion about my death. They want the police to keep thinking it was an accident.

Would Link have looked for anything you were working on?

Yes. My laptop and some files and papers were on my desk. He would have taken them when he picked up my dog.

Wouldn't he have searched through your laptop?

Everything on it is encrypted. And he doesn't have my password. He probably tried to access it, but I doubt he got anywhere.

I swished my feet in the water. When I was alive, I wouldn't have wanted my feet in that dark, murky water. Now, it didn't matter whether the water was dirty or pristine. I couldn't feel it anyway.

I glanced at Teddy and rested my hand on top of his. When he looked at me, I said, *Has it been so awful being stuck here?*

He gave a sad smile. *It would have been . . . without you.*

I squeezed his hand. *And you. Do you ever wonder about what's waiting for us over there, on the other side of the veil?*

Only every day, he said. *In fiction, our dearly departed loved ones are lined up to welcome us with open arms. I lost both my parents before I graduated from college. It would be amazing to see them again.*

I hope that's true, I said. *There are people over there I've missed. My grandparents, aunts and uncles, friends. I wonder if our pets are there. When I was a kid, my very best friend was my dog, Brandy. Even more than Kiki. I was completely devastated when he died of old age. I want to see Brandy again. I hope he's there.*

Our dogs bring joy every day we have them, Teddy said.

Brandy was joyful. That's for sure. The way he would burst through the front door when I opened it and jump all over me before I could get inside. That's great love in doggie form.

He slipped an arm around my shoulders, and I snuggled close. Looking up at him, I said softly, *Staying here wouldn't be so bad if I still had you.*

Chapter 29

Roz left the package at home. No point in carrying it around until it was time to do something with it.

She and Kiki were waiting for us, and Kiki seemed agitated.

What's up? I asked as soon as I saw her worried face.

"I'm not sure, but I think someone's following me."

What? Who's following you? I asked.

"I don't know. It was a black SUV. I went to Starbucks this morning. At first, I didn't think anything of it when it pulled away from the curb as I left my driveway, but, when I was driving home after getting my coffee, I glanced in the rearview mirror and it looked like the same car. I thought I was being silly, but, just in case, I took the long way home and stopped at Gelson's for some grapes. When I got back in my car and pulled out of the Gelson's parking lot, I saw it again. It let a couple of cars get in front of it, but I could still see it when I got to my house."

Is it out there now? I asked.

"I don't think so. I checked a couple of times and didn't see it. But . . . what do they want?"

I think maybe when Ethan didn't find Laurel's phone at his house he decided to branch out, Teddy said. *You'd be the logical next step.*

"That gives me the creeps," Kiki said with a shudder. "I wish Mike were here."

"Where is he?" Roz asked.

"He had a surgery this morning. I texted him about the SUV, and he'll come over when he can."

That makes me nervous, I said. *We know how dangerous Ethan is. Kiki, I think Teddy and I are going to stay with you. I don't know what we can do if he shows up—*

"You can tell me," Roz said. "I can call the police."

"But what would you tell them?" Kiki asked.

"That I had a call from you," Roz said, "and you were worried someone was breaking into your house."

That's a pretty good plan, Roz, I said. *Excuse me. I'll be right back.*

I thought myself out onto the street in front of Kiki's, but there was no sign of a black SUV. In an instant I was back in the house.

Roz, I said, *I don't think you should be here. The SUV isn't out there right now, but we don't want to take the chance that it drives by and sees your car and adds you to the list of people they think might have had contact with Laurel.*

She frowned. "But I—" She moved to the window and looked out at the street. "I don't like it, but I see your point. Especially since I do have the evidence."

"Where did you put it? You know, in case, um, something happens and we need to find it?" Kiki asked.

"You mean something like Ethan knocks me off?"

"I'm sorry," Kiki said, looking sheepish. "I didn't mean anything by it."

"Doesn't matter. Because you're right. You don't want the secret to die with me."

Now you're just being morbid, I said.

Roz laughed. "That's just me. Don't worry. I can take care of myself."

We're sure you can, Teddy said. *But just in case why don't you tell us where you stashed it.*

"Wouldn't you like to know?" Roz said, then flopped a hand at us.

"Just kidding. I hid it in the blue tea tin in my reading room. Under the tea."

"Ingenious," Kiki said.

"Thank you," Roz said. "I thought so."

So, really, Roz. Will you leave now?

"Yes, as long as you promise to keep me posted about what's going on."

You'll be the first to know, I said. *Because you have the evidence. We couldn't do it without you.*

Roz gave Kiki a surprise hug, and waved goodbye to me and Teddy. I followed her out and scanned the street to make sure no one was paying attention. We couldn't let anything stop us now.

After she was gone, Kiki and Teddy and I lounged around the pool all afternoon.

Teddy and I stayed out after Kiki went inside to shower and change clothes. It was comforting to be out by the pool and could almost make us forget the circumstances that had brought us here.

When I heard the doorbell ring, I nudged Teddy and we appeared inside to find Ethan standing in the open doorway. I held Teddy's arm to keep him from attacking Ethan, not that he could have done any damage to the murderer.

"What do you need, Ethan?" Kiki asked, glancing at us.

"Oh, uh, nothing. I just wanted to check up on you. I know you were close to Laurel, and I miss her so much. I was sure you were missing her too. It was a shame what happened to her."

"Yeah, a real shame," Kiki said. "You didn't seem that upset the day she died, though. So I'm not sure how genuine your words are now. But, whatever. I'm fine, but I have things to do. Thanks for stopping by."

Ethan grabbed her arm, which Kiki immediately jerked away. Ethan held up his hands and backed away. "Sorry. I just . . . I wanted to ask you something."

Kiki put her hands on her hips and glared at him. "What?"

"I just wondered. I haven't been able to find Laurel's phone. I wondered if you might have it."

Kiki looked at me and Teddy over Ethan's shoulder. Ethan turned to see what she was looking at but, of course, he saw nothing.

"Why would I have her phone?" she asked Ethan. "It should have been with her."

"That's what I thought," Ethan said, "but it wasn't anywhere. I thought maybe she'd left it here accidentally or something."

"No. Sorry. I can't help you." Kiki started to close the door, indicating to Ethan that he should leave. "Now, I really have to get ready. Mike's coming over and we're going out."

Ethan barely concealed his anger, but ducked his head and said, "Okay. Sorry to have bothered you."

The three of us stood in Kiki's front doorway and watched him drive away. In a black SUV.

"Oh, my God," she said. "It was Ethan following me."

Troubling.

We need to get the evidence to the police sooner rather than later, Teddy said. *I don't think he believed you. I wouldn't put it past him to break in here.*

Kiki looked scared. "He's a killer. Should I get a gun or something?"

Maybe you should have Mike stay here, I said. *Or you should stay with him. I don't think you should be here alone while he's still out there.*

I don't, either, Teddy said.

"Mike's going to be here soon, and I still have to take a shower," Kiki said. "Don't leave, okay?"

We're not going anywhere, I said. *Go on and get ready.* Before she left the room, I said, *Nice dig at Ethan by the way.*

Kiki smiled. "Wasn't it?"

Chapter 30

Mike hadn't heard from Link by the time he got to Kiki's. Teddy suggested calling him again. This time, Link answered.

Mike put the phone on speaker as he explained that he was a friend of Teddy's and needed to meet with Link.

"How do you know Teddy?" Link sounded guarded.

"I met him recently. He left something with me that he wants you to have."

"What is it?"

"I'd prefer not to discuss it over the phone. Can we meet?"

There was silence on the line. "I'm not sure that's such a good idea," Link finally said.

"It's important. You'll want to hear what I have to say," Mike said. "Look, we can meet somewhere public. How about a bar? You could be sitting at the bar, and I could take a seat next to you. No one would suspect we were meeting."

"I suspect you," Link said. "Let me think about it. I'll get back to you." And he clicked off.

"Damn it," Mike said. "Sorry about that. Maybe I should have—"

Link's suspicious for his own safety, Teddy said. *You said all the right things. I'm sure he'll come around. Just maybe not as fast as we want him to.*

"Exactly. Not as fast as we want," Mike said. "I'm going to call him back."

And say what? Teddy asked. *Give him a little time. If we don't hear back from him in an hour, then you can call. And you can tell him I'm here.*

"He'll think I'm deranged if I tell him that."

It worked when I told Roz to contact Kiki, I added. *Teddy, you need to come up with something that only you and he would know. Maybe it will intrigue him enough to agree to a meeting.*

"It may be our only shot," Mike said.

There's something else, I said. *Ethan dropped in on Kiki this afternoon asking about the phone. He's been following her.*

"What? He was the one in the SUV you told me about? Are you okay?"

"I'm fine," she said. "Except maybe a little freaked out."

"I'm going to stay with you for a few nights. Just in case."

"That makes me feel better." Kiki patted his knee. "My hero."

"Uh, thanks? I haven't done anything yet."

"You're a hero just for offering," Kiki said and leaned over to kiss his cheek.

Mike laughed and waved her off. "I guess it's a good thing we left the phone and thumb drive with Roz."

I agree, I said. *I was worried something like this might happen. Ethan must be desperate to get his hands on my phone.*

An hour seemed like an eternity, but, when it was over, we all hovered around Mike. He took a deep breath and punched in Link's number.

"I told you, I'll let you know," were Link's first words.

"I know you're hesitant to reveal yourself," Mike said. "Teddy told me you're keeping a low profile so anyone who went after him wouldn't know about you."

"How do you—?"

"Look, Link. Teddy's death wasn't an accident. He was murdered. We know how and by whom. Teddy left something with me that you need to have. It's vital for us to meet."

There was a silence on the line so long I was worried that we'd lost the connection. Finally, Link said, "I don't want to meet here. There's a coffee shop close to my house. I think we can have privacy there. When do you want to meet?"

"As soon as possible," Mike said. "We could be there in an hour. Text me the address."

Mike looked at us. "This is getting real. I'm a doctor, not a detective. How did I get myself into this?"

Kiki slipped an arm around him. "For me. You did it for me."

"I did. And I don't regret it at all."

Chapter 31

We arrived fifteen minutes early and found a U-shaped booth in a back corner of the coffee shop. Teddy spotted Link when he walked in and gestured to Mike, who waved Link over.

Mike introduced himself to Link, and then introduced Kiki. There was awkward silence for a moment. Link was apprehensive, running his hand through his hair and glancing nervously around the room.

"You weren't very clear earlier. How do you know . . . did you know . . . Teddy?" Link asked.

Mike cleared his throat. "I met him through, uh, friends. Look, that's not important. What is important is this." He slid his hand across the table toward Link. When he pulled back his hand, the thumb drive sat next to Link's water glass. It was Mike's turn to glance nervously around the coffee shop, but it didn't appear that anyone had taken notice.

"What's—?" Link started.

"Teddy said to get this to you, and you'd know what to do with it. He said it had to do with something he was investigating."

Link palmed the thumb drive and pocketed it.

"Okay. You said Teddy was murdered and you know who did it. How do you know that?"

"Someone took a video. That person was also killed."

Link opened his mouth to answer, but before he could, a server appeared to bring their drinks and take their orders, adding "I'll be back in a few minutes with your order" over her shoulder as she left.

"So, wait," Link said. "There were two murders? Are they related?"

"Yes," Mike said. "Look, I don't know what's on that thumb drive, but Teddy thought you needed to see it."

"Yeah," Link said. "I'll check it out and see what needs to be done after. What do you know?"

"We know it has something to do with smuggling relics or artifacts or something from South America."

"Hmm. Yeah. Teddy was trying to run down sources and methods. There was a shipping company he suspected—"

"He was right about that," Mike said.

"It was Palmer-Knight Shipping International," Kiki said. "My best friend was Laurel Palmer. Her husband ran Palmer-Knight."

"Was?" Link pinned Kiki with a sharp look.

"Yes. *Was*," Kiki spat out. "He killed her."

"And he's the one who killed Teddy?"

Mike nodded.

"So, there's a video . . . " Link ran a hand through his hair.

"Of Ethan Palmer and Jeff Knight murdering Teddy," Kiki said.

"Do you have it?"

"Yes. We're going to turn it over to the police. Teddy can't rest until they prove his death wasn't an accident," Kiki said.

"Teddy can't rest?" Link asked.

Teddy stood behind Link and laid his hands on his friend's shoulders. Of course, Link was unaware of Teddy's presence.

"What do you mean he can't rest?"

"Oh," Kiki reddened and put a hand to her mouth. "I didn't mean anything by it. I just figured he wouldn't be able to rest easy without people knowing the truth."

The server took that moment to return with plates of food. Which no one touched.

Ask him about Buck, Teddy said. When Mike looked confused, Teddy added, *He's my dog.*

"How's Buck?" Mike asked.

"How do you know about Buck?"

"Teddy mentioned you had him."

Link turned in his seat to face Mike. "Teddy couldn't have told you that. I didn't pick up Buck until after Teddy was dead." Link stood. "Something's not right here." He grabbed the lightweight jacket he'd brought with him.

You have to tell him we're here, Teddy said. *Quick, before he leaves.*

"Teddy's right," Kiki said. "You have to tell him."

Link looked from Kiki to Mike and back again.

Mike wiped a hand down his face. "Look, there's more, but you're not gonna believe it."

"But at least give us a chance to explain," Kiki said. She reached out her hand. "Please."

After a moment of indecision, Link slid back into the booth, sitting stiffly. Like he was there against his will. "Okay. What's the deal?"

"All right, but I know you're gonna jump up and run out of here when we tell you," Kiki said, squeezing Mike's hand.

Link glowered at Kiki like she was missing a few puzzle pieces.

"Can you do that thing where you move the glass or something?" Kiki asked me. "Maybe it'll make it easier to explain."

You should tell him first. When he doesn't believe you, then I can show him.

"Who are you talking to?" Link asked Kiki sharply, obviously losing patience.

Kiki looked helplessly at Mike. "You tell him."

"Link, man, this is going to sound strange. Believe me. I didn't believe it at first. I didn't really believe it until I saw them with my own eyes."

"Saw who?" Link asked.

"Teddy . . . and Laurel Palmer." Mike sighed. "I saw them for the first time about a week ago."

When Link picked up his jacket again, Kiki put her hand on his arm. "Wait. I know how this sounds. And it's crazy. But it's true. Teddy and Laurel are here with us. Right now." She indicated the seemingly empty spot in the center of the U-shaped booth where Teddy and I were sitting.

"You guys are crazy," Link snarled. "None of this is funny. I don't know what you're trying to pull—"

"Laurel, do something!" Kiki cried.

I picked up the nearest water glass and set it back down in front of Link. Whose eyes bugged out of his head.

Teddy slid a fork toward Link until it touched his hand. Link pushed back against the booth as far as he could get from the table. "What . . . what—"

"Laurel's the glass and Teddy sent the fork," Mike said.

"They came to us for help after they were killed," Kiki said, her words running together in her haste to get them all out. "They're stuck here until we prove they were murdered."

"What . . . what—" Link was still sputtering, and Kiki laughed nervously.

"I told you that you wouldn't believe it," Mike said.

"You don't have to worry about them," Kiki said. "They won't hurt you. So don't be scared of them."

Link ran a hand through his hair, his eyes not quite as wild as they'd been when glass and utensil moved.

"Whoa," he said, and summoned the server to request a coffee refill.

A second server instantaneously arrived with the coffee pot and refilled all the cups. Link sat silently, hands around the mug in a death grip.

"Are you okay?" Kiki asked, her face reflecting concern that this was too much for him.

Link sniffed. "You have to realize how all this sounds, right?"

"Of course, we do," Mike said.

Teddy and I watched, unable to add anything to the conversation that Link would be able to hear.

After a moment, Link lifted his mug and took a sip of his coffee. "So, what happens now?"

"We give the video to the police," Mike said, "and hope they follow up. Do you think there would be anything on that thumb drive that could be helpful to them?"

"I won't know until I look at it," Link said.

"What do you think is on there?" Kiki asked.

"I'm guessing any evidence Teddy collected."

Tell him it's video from the truck yard. I managed to sneak into the yard one night when I followed Ethan Palmer from a restaurant, and he thoughtfully didn't close the chain-link gate behind him. Most of the lights in the yard were located around one of the buildings, so I was able to get pretty close and record him and Jeff Knight unloading one of the big rigs. One particular crate was a bingo moment. Although I wasn't close enough to see the detail of the pieces, I could tell they were South American figures that they handled very carefully.

Link had been watching Mike and Kiki as their attention was focused on the empty area of the booth. "What's going on?" he asked.

"Sorry about that," Mike said. "Teddy said there's a video of Palmer and Knight unloading some artifacts."

"No kidding! Anything else?" Link followed Mike's eyes to where he supposed we were to be found.

Yeah. I waited for Palmer and his pals to leave, then pried open the door of the warehouse where they'd stashed the crates. Voilà! All I had to do was pull out the pieces and video them. Link can match up the items with records of stolen goods. Whether they're listed as stolen or not, it's illegal to smuggle Pre-Columbian art and South American antiquities into our country under the

1970 UNESCO Convention and various other U.S. laws. Not to mention the NSPA and CPIA—

"What's the NSPA?" Kiki said.

"The National Stolen Property Act," Link said, shocked as it became clear to him that Teddy's ghost was really sitting in the booth.

He took another gulp of his coffee and ran his hand through his hair. "Wow. All I can say is wow."

So, how's Buck? Teddy asked with a chuckle. *Does he miss me?*

Kiki laughed. "Teddy wants to know if Buck misses him."

Link shook his head. "This is all too much. He... I'm talking to a ghost." He dropped his head into his hands, then looked up. "Tell him Buck's sad, but Lisa and I are helping him get over it."

"You can tell him yourself," Kiki said. "He's sitting right there."

"Maybe so, but it's harder than you think talking to empty air."

"No, not harder than I think, because I went through the same thing when Laurel first contacted me, and I couldn't see her. I get it."

She looked at Teddy and whispered, "Who's Lisa?"

"I'm right here," Link said. "She's my wife."

"Oh, sorry," Kiki said, patting her cheeks as they turned a charming shade of bright red.

The café was nearly empty by this point. None of them had noticed anyone who might be trying to listen in to their conversation, but Link swept the area with his eyes. Feeling safe, he picked up his jacket and stood. "Look. I'm gonna go home and see what all he's got on this drive. Let me know what the police say."

"Maybe you should make another copy or two of it, just in case," Mike said. "Then hide them somewhere."

"That's a great idea," Link said. "I'll take care of it."

After Link left, the four of us discussed our next move.

Teddy and I should go tell Roz what's happening. She'll be wondering. What about you? I asked Kiki.

"Mike and I are going home. We need to figure out who to give your phone to. You know, the police, the FBI, or some other agency. Which one would be the proper choice since this involves smuggling artifacts?"

Yeah, but they won't know about the smuggling when you give them the video. They don't know about the thumb drive, so I would think at this point it's a police matter. What do you think, Teddy?

I agree. The police are the ones who would investigate a murder.

Chapter 32

Roz had missed the meeting with Link because she had two customers lined up that afternoon. When Teddy and I arrived in her reception area, we could hear quiet voices coming from her reading room, so we settled on the red velvet settee to wait.

Roz noticed us as she ushered the sniffling woman toward the front door and nodded imperceptibly at us.

"There, there, Mrs. Janks," the medium said soothingly. "It was a very successful reading. Now you know your husband is watching over you and maybe you won't be so lonely anymore."

"Thank you, Madam Rosalind," Mrs. Janks responded. "I'm so happy to know he's not really gone. I feel so close to him now."

Roz laid a comforting hand on her customer's back as she held open the door, then closed it after Mrs. Janks had stepped outside.

"So, what happened?"

It went better than I hoped, I said. *Of course, Teddy and I had to move some tableware around to get our point across.*

"That must have freaked him out."

Oh, yeah. You could say that.

I think it was when I described what was on the thumb drive that he finally had to let go and just believe, Teddy added.

"What now?"

Now Kiki has to take my phone to the police, I said.

"But what about—"

Before Roz could finish her question, her cell buzzed, and she held up a just-a-minute finger before she answered it.

The color drained out of her face. Something was wrong. After a short call, she said, "That was Kiki. Someone broke into her house. Everything was trashed."

Oh, my God, I moaned. Kiki loved her house. This would be a blow.

Teddy interrupted my thoughts. *Is she okay?*

"Mike was with her, and they called the police."

That was alarming. *We need to get over there before she talks to the police*, I said.

"Why? What's wrong?" Roz asked.

This complicates things. If she tells the police she suspects Ethan, they'll want to know why, and she'll have to tell them he wants my phone, but Kiki's not supposed to know what's on it yet. She needs to be careful what she says.

I stood and pulled Teddy up beside me. *We have to go, Roz. I'll let you know what happens.*

It only took the blink of an eye for us to be standing in Kiki's foyer. Kiki and Mike were righting upended furniture.

Should you be doing that? I asked.

Kiki whirled around. "Oh, Laurel. Look what he did to my home!" She had tears in her eyes.

I know. But maybe you shouldn't touch anything before the police get here. They'll want to take crime scene photos.

Kiki looked around her at the destruction and dropped her head into her hands.

Mike stood helplessly, not sure what to say. He pulled her into his arms, and she cried softly against his chest.

Listen, you guys, I said. *When the police get here, you shouldn't tell them it was Ethan.*

"Why not?" Kiki lifted her head and looked at me. "We know it was him."

I'm sure it was, but you haven't given the phone to the police yet. There will be a lot of questions about how you know it was Ethan. You'll have to tell them that he was here looking for my phone. Since we still have it, it won't make sense that he destroyed your house trying to find his wife's phone. They don't know what's on it, and presumably you don't know what's on it either at this point.

"What do we do then?" Mike asked.

Just tell the police you came home and found it like this and that you don't know anyone who'd want to do this to you. Later, maybe tomorrow, you can take the phone in and give the police the story about how you'd forgotten you had it but when you looked at it you saw something they needed to see. You can point out that it's Ethan and Jeff, but you don't know who the third guy is.

If I know Ethan, I said, *he'd have been careful and worn gloves, so the police shouldn't find fingerprints. After they see what's on the phone, then they might possibly connect the dots. You have to play it cool and stick to the plan.*

"And I can tell them that he came by here asking if I'd seen your phone, and that I think he's been following me."

Yep. That should point them in the right direction. You can take the phone to the police in the morning. Roz still has it, so can you stop by her shop and get it?

"We can do that," Mike said. "But you're spending the night at my house," he said to Kiki.

We heard car doors outside. The police had arrived.

Teddy and I stood out of the way in the foyer and observed the officers investigating the scene. Kiki was wonderful. She didn't mention anything about knowing who the culprit was. I'd been holding my breath there for a minute, worried she'd blurt out something inappropriate.

I wouldn't hold my breath that they're going to find anything, I said.

Not today anyway, Teddy added.

Kiki looked like she'd lost her best friend. I know. Stupid pun. I couldn't blame her. It would be very unsettling and upsetting to have your sanctuary invaded. If you can't feel safe at home . . .

Kiki went up to her bedroom to pack so she could stay at Mike's for a while. I followed her up and sat on her bed. A single tear that escaped and slid down her cheek broke my heart. And made me angry. It wasn't enough that Ethan murdered me, he had to terrorize Kiki, as well?

I'm sorry, Kiki.

"It's okay. It's not your fault," she said, not looking at me.

I patted the bed beside me, but she couldn't hear the action, so I said, *Come sit down.* I wanted to offer what little comfort I was able to, and she needed to know that I was there for her. Except I wasn't really there. So, big help *I* was.

After she finished packing her Vuitton travel tote, she dropped it on the floor and sank down on the bed beside me.

She looked at me with red-rimmed eyes, then sighed heavily and dropped her head.

It's gonna be all right, sweetie, I said, hoping it were true.

"I know," she said, but she couldn't disguise the dejection in her voice.

I should have left her out of this. It wasn't fair for her life to be impacted by what happened to me.

When I looked up, she was watching me.

"Are *you* okay?" she asked.

Don't worry about me. I'm just sorry I got you into this.

"I'm fine. Pretty upset at the moment, but I'm tough." She raised her arms in a weightlifter pose to show her muscles. "See?"

I laughed.

She cleared her throat. "There's something I've been meaning to ask you. Have you, um, have you ever seen . . . " She looked away from me as if embarrassed.

I didn't understand for a moment, but then a light bulb went on. *Have I seen Arnie?* I asked gently.

"Yeah." She fiddled with her fingers, still not looking at me.

No, hon, I haven't. I haven't seen any other spirits except Teddy. I wished I had a better answer for her. I felt at a loss for a moment, then added, *But, if I do run into him, I'll tell him you miss him and that you love him.*

"Thank you." Her eyes filled. She stood and picked up her tote. "But please don't tell Mike I asked you. I don't want to hurt his feelings."

I won't. I don't think he'd mind, though, that you still care about Arnie.

"I know. He'd understand." She started toward the door. "Let's go back down."

With a sense of anxiety over the monumental task of presenting the police with the iPhone video and actually getting them to believe Kiki's story, we said our goodbyes and went our separate ways.

Teddy and I popped back in on Roz to let her know what happened at Kiki's. And to make sure she'd be ready with the phone when Kiki arrived in the morning.

Chapter 33

Teddy and I returned to the dock, both of us nervous. The end was in sight. Tomorrow was the big day. Nothing could go wrong now.

Could it?

That one little doubt was enough to keep us from basking in the joy that tomorrow would surely bring.

We sat side by side on the dock, dangling our feet in the water. Behind us, on the other side of the dock, sat my husband's yacht . . . or boat, as he called it. Funny that neither Teddy nor I had considered going aboard her. I stood and approached her bow, leaning over to touch the words in blue and white script: *SURPRISE.*

Why did he name it "Surprise?" Teddy asked. *I would probably have chosen something like "Laurel's Dream." Something personal anyway.*

It was a big joke to him. Like, Surprise! You didn't think I'd be super-rich, did you? I shook my head. *It should have tipped me off to what an egomaniac he was.*

Was he already rich when you married him? Teddy asked.

Yep. Already had it all. Even the boat. I floated up onto the deck. *Want to see inside?*

Teddy appeared at my side for the tour. He was blown away at the opulence. The boat had three bedrooms, or staterooms, whatever you call them. Gleaming teak floors and cabinets, marble countertops in the galley, which was big enough to be called a kitchen, gold fittings in the bathrooms, sable throws on the beds, although who needs a fur throw in Southern California?

We reclined on one of the beds, and Teddy drew me into his arms. We both felt safe and comforted that way.

Will you still want to be with me on the other side? I asked, lifting my head off his shoulder to gaze into his eyes.

He smiled a reassuring smile and leaned in to kiss me.

For eternity, he answered.

He held me tightly and we kissed until our bodies dissolved into mist and spiraled together, floating in the air, our souls inextricably bound and our happiness boundless.

As our misty bodies resumed their ghostly forms, we lay side by side and remembered our journey and spoke excitedly about being free of this earthly plane, the people we couldn't wait to see again, the love that would envelop us when we went into the light.

Only then did we truly feel the joy that tomorrow would surely bring.

Chapter 34

It was decided that Roz wouldn't join us when we delivered the phone to the police. No one wanted to have to explain what her part was in all this. So, it was just Kiki and Mike and me and Teddy who walked into the precinct and asked to speak to someone regarding the death of Teddy Rule.

After waiting a few minutes, a youngish black officer appeared. "I'm Officer Kennedy. Can I help you?" he asked.

Kiki looked nervously at Mike, while Teddy and I hovered nearby.

"We have some information on Teddy Rule's death," he said.

"Teddy Rule . . . " Officer Kennedy seemed to contemplate that for a moment. "Mr. Rule's death was an accident," he finally responded.

"No," Mike said. "Actually, it wasn't."

Not giving anything away, the officer subtly shifted his stance and his gaze sharpened. "It was ruled that his drowning was accidental." He watched Mike carefully. "You have reason to suspect otherwise?"

"We do," Mike said. "And we have proof, if you can just give us a minute."

Officer Kennedy ushered us all down a hall to a stark room with a heavy table and three chairs. If I had to guess, this was an interrogation room. When the officer and Kiki and Mike were all seated, Officer Kennedy said, "So. Your proof?"

Mike slid the phone across the table. "There's video on there you'll want to see."

· 163 ·

"Your phone?" Officer Kennedy asked.

"No. It belongs . . . belonged to Laurel Palmer. Whom we believe was also murdered."

"Hang on. Don't get ahead of yourself there."

"May I?" Mike asked and picked up the phone. He keyed in my passcode and pulled up the video. "See for yourself."

Officer Kennedy silently watched the video, then watched it two more times. "You've been sitting on this for weeks."

"It's my fault," Kiki said, her voice cracking. "I found it."

"You just found it?" the officer asked.

"No. I found it the morning of Laurel's death."

"Laurel?"

"Laurel Palmer. It's her phone."

"Why didn't you give it to her husband?"

"He's the one who killed her! And he killed Teddy Rule, too. It's right there on the video."

"Then why didn't you come to the police right away?"

"I would have, but I didn't watch the video until recently."

"So, you sat on the phone for weeks, and you didn't give it back to her husband?"

"I told you. He's the one who killed her."

"This isn't making any sense."

Kiki looked down at her hands, twined in her lap, and whispered, "I'm sorry."

Officer Kennedy leaned back in his chair and crossed his arms.

Mike reached over and squeezed Kiki's hand. "Go on. It's okay. Tell him everything."

Kiki drew in a deep breath, not looking at the officer. "I found Laurel's phone on my porch when I opened the door that morning. The morning she died. I put it in my purse. We were going to have lunch that day and I would give it to her then." She took her hand back from Mike and pushed a strand of her hair behind her ear. "When Mike and I got to her house, I knocked but there was no answer, so I used my key and stuck my head in and called her name, but she didn't answer so I went in. That's when I saw her. She was lying at the bottom of the stairs, and I . . . " she stifled a sob. My heart went out to her.

Kiki composed herself and went on. "And there was blood. And then Ethan came down the stairs and—"

"Who's Ethan?" Officer Kennedy asked. He'd leaned forward again, and his forearms were resting on the table.

"Ethan is Laurel's husband. He seemed upset that we were there and said we should go. That he'd take care of everything. I told Mike to call 911 and Ethan said he'd already done it, so Mike disconnected the call. When 911 called back, because, you know, they do that, they told him they didn't have any calls regarding that address and that the dispatcher was sending an ambulance."

"When Ethan heard the sirens, he seemed upset," Mike said.

"And he never said a word about Laurel as she lay there on the floor," Kiki said. "Like he didn't even care."

Officer Kennedy pinched the bridge of his nose.

"And he came to my house asking if I'd found Laurel's phone," Kiki said.

"But you didn't give it to him."

"No. Because it was odd that he would come to me. I mean, why was it important for him to find her phone? Not only that, I think he's been following me. I'd thought a black SUV was following me the day before, and then, when Ethan was leaving my house, he got in a black SUV."

"You still haven't said why you held onto the phone for so long," Officer Kennedy said.

"Oh. With Laurel's death and all, it slipped my mind. I was reminded of it when Ethan came looking for it. That's what made me wonder why it was so important, so Mike and I searched what was on it—"

"It wasn't locked?"

"It was, but Laurel and I knew each other's passwords. We were best friends."

"Okay. Go on."

"That's about it. When we saw the video, I knew why Ethan wanted it."

"Did you know Mr. Rule?"

Kiki looked at Mike in alarm, not sure what she should say.

"The video after the one you looked at," Mike said. "Laurel said a guy came up to her at the marina. His name was Teddy Rule. Then she said she just saw her husband murder him."

The officer picked up the phone and accessed the second video, which backed up Mike's story.

I'm so glad I did that, I said, and Kiki glanced at me and nodded imperceptibly.

Officer Kennedy stood. "I need to get the footage verified. Don't leave town. We'll want to talk to you again." He opened the interrogation room door and indicated that Mike and Kiki should go. He followed them to the front desk and instructed them to leave their contact information with the desk sergeant.

As Kiki and Mike were about to leave, she called out, "Officer Kennedy?"

He turned back. "Yes?"

"My home was broken into last night. The police came. Maybe it was related?"

"Was anything taken?"

"No. Just things thrown around like someone was looking for something. I stayed with Mike last night because I was afraid to stay there."

"Okay. We'll check to see if there's a connection." He started to walk away, then paused. "Thanks for coming in. We'll take it from here."

Outside the precinct building, Kiki turned to me. "Are you guys coming over? We can talk about what happened."

I looked at Teddy questioningly.

Sounds good to me, he said.

Sure. We'll meet you there.

Teddy and I watched them drive away, since it would take us significantly less time to get to Kiki's than it would Kiki and Mike. I took Teddy's hand, ready to go, when I saw a familiar black SUV pull away from its parking spot on the street and head the same way as Kiki and Mike had gone. Teddy and I followed until it was obvious the SUV was following our friends. I willed myself into the passenger seat of the SUV and then back out again.

It's Ethan, I told Teddy.

We need to tell Kiki and Mike, Teddy said.

Kiki gasped when we popped up in the backseat. Before she could ask why we were there, I said, *Ethan's following you.*

Do you have any guns at your house? Teddy asked.

Kiki looked at Mike in alarm. "What do we do?"

Mike glanced in the rearview mirror, trying to spot the SUV. Sure enough, it was two cars back.

"Call the police," Mike said, and Kiki pulled out her cell phone and Officer Kennedy's card.

When the officer answered, Kiki said, "Ethan Palmer is following us. I'm scared what he's going to do."

The officer said he'd send a car over and that Kiki and Mike should go inside and make sure the doors were locked, so when we arrived at Kiki's, Mike drove straight into the garage and closed the door after they were inside.

The doors of the house were already locked, and Kiki clutched Mike's arm, her eyes big and frightened.

"We do have a gun," she said. "Arnie kept it for protection. It's in a drawer in the bedside table."

You guys go upstairs and get it, I said. *You probably won't have to use it, but if Ethan tries anything before the police get here, it'll make you feel more secure. Teddy and I will watch Ethan.*

Teddy and I willed ourselves into the yard just as Ethan was climbing out of the SUV. He had a determined look on his face as he stalked up to the front door. He jiggled the doorknob and then banged on the door.

"Come on, Kiki. Open up. I need to talk to you."

When he didn't get an answer, he crossed around to the backdoor and tried the lock. He banged his fist against the door. "Why were you at the police station?"

He rounded back to the front door and stood with his hands on his hips. "Kiki!" he yelled, then picked up a large rock that bordered the walkway and heaved it through one of the vertical windows that framed the door, then reached his hand inside trying to reach the lock. It only took a moment before he'd managed to unlock the door and push it open. The security alarm started to blare as Ethan stomped into the house. "I want that phone, Kiki. Give it to me and I'll leave you alone. I know you have it. You're the only one Laurel would trust with it."

Ethan headed for the kitchen and searched the dining room and family room. Before starting upstairs, he grabbed one of the fireplace pokers.

Kiki, I yelled. *Ethan's on his way up. Block the door if you can.*

Teddy and I raced to stand with them. I was relieved to see that Mike had the gun and was loading some cartridges into it. He clicked the gun shut and stood facing the bedroom door.

Ethan rattled the doorknob and banged his shoulder into it. One more good slam and the door would give way.

The sound of sirens and slamming car doors caused Ethan to back away. I flew through the door and watched him peer over the banister trying to see out the front window. He rushed down the stairs and through the kitchen, dropping the poker as he flung open the backdoor.

An officer stuck his head in the open door and called out "Police!"

Guns drawn, he and his partner cautiously entered. "Is anyone here?"

Kiki and Mike timidly appeared at the top of the stairs. "Is he gone?" Kiki asked.

He went out the backdoor, I said.

"I think we heard the backdoor," Mike said, and one of the officers headed through the kitchen.

The officer came back into the foyer holding the poker in a gloved hand.

The cops gathered everyone in the family room to take statements. They offered to have a car outside to keep an eye out in case Ethan returned, and Kiki quickly accepted the offer.

"Are you going to arrest him?" Mike asked.

"We'll pick him up. You should be okay now."

"Do you think you can find him?" Kiki asked. "He knows you'll be looking for him."

"We can get his license information and put out a BOLO. Don't worry. We'll get him."

Chapter 35

Teddy and I felt a sense of peace. It was almost over. Ethan would be apprehended, and with the video evidence there'd at least be a trial. I had no question that Ethan would get a high-powered lawyer, but there was almost surely a reason for them to investigate my death as well. Teddy and I could leave now.

We sat on the dock, somehow our go-to place, dangling our feet in the water and holding hands.

I'm not sure I really believed this day would ever come, Teddy said.

I slipped under his arm. *It seemed like an impossible mountain to climb. But we did it.*

What happens now, do you think? he asked.

I don't know. Will we know when it's going to happen? Will we feel it?

In a futile gesture, Teddy brushed at a leaf on the dock. *And how long do you think it'll take? Do we have to wait until Ethan and Jeff are found guilty and sentenced?*

I shrugged. *I don't know, but I hope not. With appeals, it could take years. It would be unfair to leave us here. We gave the police the proof they needed to be able to make a case against Ethan and Jeff. What else do we have to do?*

I stood and started to pace. *What if the evidence gets tossed on a technicality? Ethan will undoubtedly argue that the video was manufactured.*

When Link hears about Ethan's arrest, or when Mike tells him about it, he'll be able to provide a motive for the killings.

Teddy joined me and pulled me into his arms. *We've done everything we could. Now we have to wait. It won't be so bad, will it? If we're together?*

No. As long as we're together. I didn't mention the psychic's prediction that we wouldn't be.

Out of spite, we spent the night on Ethan's yacht. If I could sink it, I would.

·   ·   ·

Teddy and I checked in on Roz in the morning and filled her in on the events of yesterday.

"I had a feeling everything would go well," she said.

A feeling feeling or just wishful thinking? I asked. *Because, psychic and all.*

She laughed. "More a hope."

Can you call Kiki? I asked. *I think . . . I hope . . . Teddy and I will be moving on soon now that we've provided the police with proof of the murders. If we are leaving, we want to be with you all to say goodbye.*

"You're leaving?" A look of surprise crossed Roz's face. "I guess I didn't think about that."

I laughed. *All good things must end. And I could be wrong.*

Roz grabbed her phone and called Kiki. "They'll be right here."

I didn't allow myself to dwell on leaving these people behind. There would be time for that when the moment came to say our goodbyes.

It's been fun, hasn't it? I asked Roz.

She grinned. "Slightly more fun than a poke in the eye with a sharp stick." Rolling her eyes, she added, "Only slightly."

It seemed like an eternity before Kiki and Mike arrived, although it was probably twenty minutes. The first words out of Kiki's mouth were, "They caught him!"

"The police picked him up in San Diego," Mike added. "They think he was on his way to the Mexican border."

"The weasel," Kiki said.

It didn't surprise me. It wouldn't surprise me that Ethan would take the easy way out.

"They said he had twenty thousand in cash on him," Mike said.

I'm sure he has offshore accounts, as well, I said. *He probably planned to fly to the Caymans from Mexico. I wonder if Jeff's on the run, as well.*

"We should find out about that before long," Mike said. "The police will probably try to get them to turn on each other. I let Link know what was happening, and he's going to keep an eye out for the best time to come forward with the evidence about the smuggling operation. I think Ethan will have a tough time getting out of this."

"How do you feel?" Kiki asked me.

I glanced at Teddy and took his hand. *I feel happy . . . and sad.*

And excited and nervous, Teddy added.

You know what this means, don't you? I addressed Kiki. At her questioning look, I said, *We'll be leaving soon. Going into the light.* I paused and glanced again at Teddy. *Hopefully.*

"No!" Kiki looked stricken. "You can't go. I don't want to lose you."

"They have to," Roz said softly. "Spirits aren't meant to hang around the physical world. If they're still here, it means something isn't right. Don't you want them to cross over to where they're supposed to be?"

Kiki wiped at a tear that was slipping down her cheek. "But I love you."

I love you, too. All of you. Teddy and I, well, we couldn't have done this without you.

"When will you leave?" Kiki asked. "Is it right now?"

We don't know how this works, Teddy said. *But we think it could be soon, and we wanted to say a proper goodbye to you all.*

Roz, I said, *this all started with you. If you hadn't been able to see me, if you had ignored my pleas for help . . .*

"You didn't give me much choice," she replied. "You threatened to haunt me forever if I didn't."

Well, you were hesitant at first, I said, grinning. *I had to have an ace in the hole.*

"I have to admit it's been an interesting experience." She started to speak again, but her voice broke. "I'm glad I could help."

And, Mike, Teddy said. *Your help has been invaluable.*

Those wading boots! I broke in with a laugh.

You accepted us, despite your skepticism, Teddy continued. *I wish I'd been able to know you when I was alive. We could have been friends.*

"We could have double dated!" Kiki said.

I'm sorry you had to be the one to find me, Kiki, I said. *It wasn't very nice of me to ask you to do that, but it was the only way. No one would have known—*

"Seeing you like that," she said, "it was awful. Knowing that he killed you, I wanted Ethan to pay for what he did. I hope he spends the rest of his life behind bars."

I could feel my emotions bubbling to the surface, and I wanted to get all my words out while I still could. *Roz, Kiki, Mike, my heart is bursting with love for you. We're eternally grateful. I hope you realize how important you are to us. You're our heroes. Teddy and I, wherever we are, just know we'll never forget any of you. If we can, we'll be watching over you. And,* I started, tears beginning to leak from my eyes. *And we'll see you again . . . on the other side.*

"I wish I could hug you," Kiki said, wiping her eyes.

I feel your hug, I said. *I feel it in my heart.*

I took Teddy's hand and glanced up at him. *We should go now.*

I've only known you all for a minute, he said, *but I feel everything Laurel feels for you.* He made a fist and tapped his chest over his heart. *You're with me forever.*

I blew them a kiss, and we were gone.

Chapter 36

Not *gone* gone. Just gone somewhere else. Teddy wanted to stop by Link's. Even though Link couldn't see us, Buck could, and Teddy wanted one last moment with his dog. I could understand.

Link wasn't home when we appeared in the kitchen of his house. Buck was lying on the green foam dog bed. He lifted his head and whined, his tail wagging.

Teddy knelt and touched Buck's head. Buck couldn't feel it, but his big expressive doggie eyes never left Teddy's face. Teddy told Buck what a good dog he was and how much he loved him. He told him to take care of Link and pretended to ruffle Buck's ears. He told him how much he missed him and that he would see him again.

Buck seemed to understand Teddy's words, and a heartbreaking howl was his way of saying goodbye.

Teddy stood and then we were back on the dock.

Dogs are great, he said, his eyes red. *I wish . . .* He didn't finish his thought.

I know, I said. *I still miss Brandy's little face after all these years. I hope I'll see him when we cross over.*

I'm sure you will. It wouldn't be heaven if our best friends weren't there to greet us.

We settled in to wait for whatever was going to happen.

I could feel it, like a disturbance in the force. Now that the police had my phone and the evidence of Ethan's and Jeff's guilt, Teddy and I were free to go.

It was bittersweet. Despite how desperately Teddy and I wanted to cross over, I would miss our dear friends, who'd turned their lives upside down to make our wish come true. I didn't know how I would feel when we got to the other side. Would we miss everyone or would we be looking forward and not back.

In the twilight, Teddy and I stood together on the dock, somehow knowing this would be where it would happen. He leaned in and kissed me and held my hand. I was joyful, but I was also nervous, scared, worried. Teddy felt my apprehension and squeezed my fingers gently, not letting go.

It's going to be wonderful, he said.

A white light so bright we could feel the warmth emanating from it suddenly appeared at the end of the dock. Faces of our loved ones came into focus in the beautiful brilliance, and they beckoned to us. Teddy's smile was so *everything* it made my heart sing.

Holding my hand, he stepped into the light. I heard excited barking.

Brandy! I cried happily, as the little apricot bundle burst from the light to jump up and down at my feet, and my hand slipped from Teddy's as I gathered up Brandy into my arms and buried my face in his fur.

Laurel! I heard Teddy's frantic yell and looked up from my beloved dog to see the white light wink out of sight, and I was left on the dock in the dark.

Too shocked to react, I bent to let Brandy down, and stood looking at the blackness where the light had been. The light that left me behind.

I crumpled to the dock and let an ocean of tears fall.

Chapter 37

I didn't feel Brandy's dog kisses as he licked at my face. I was numb.

That was the least of it. I was scared and horrified, and unable to accept what had just happened. I vividly remembered the psychic's premonition, a premonition I'd been afraid to give credence to. And she'd been right.

I didn't move from the dock for days. I didn't go to my friends, unable to face the devastating aloneness I felt. Brandy tried to help, but even his curly apricot face wasn't enough to lift my feeling of abandonment.

Days, weeks, maybe years passed, and I didn't move. There was no comfort for me to be found. Maybe I'd spend the rest of eternity right here, on this dock, the last place I'd been with Teddy. The place the light had shined brightly and then left me behind.

Then one day I looked up into Brandy's worried face. He was confused and concerned, and he whined when he saw that I had finally noticed him. He'd never left my side, and, feeling a touch of guilt for shutting him out, I made the decision to carry on. Now, instead of Teddy and me, it would be Brandy and me.

In time, his enthusiasm jolted me out of my numb state. I let myself feel again, I smiled at Brandy's exuberance. I laughed as he carried out doggie tasks, like sniffing at imaginary smells and lifting his leg everywhere.

I gave myself a good shake and squared my shoulders, and finally accepted, to the extent I could, that Teddy was gone. How long had I been on that dock? Could have been a day, could have been a decade. There was no structure, no substance, to my existence now. No concept of time passing. Overshadowing everything was my grief, and I had to learn to bear it.

I owed it to Brandy to try to live, in a not-alive way, again. He was so happy to be with me, no matter what my mood, and I needed to show him that I was happy to be with him, too. Maybe I should check on my friends. They couldn't bring Teddy back, but my life wouldn't be barren any longer.

But did I really want to explain my failure to be with Teddy?

I willed myself to Kiki's house, but when I stood in the foyer, I was surprised not to recognize any of the people who appeared to live there. And the furniture was all wrong. Instead of sleek and elegant, in shades of white, with chrome and glass, there were now overstuffed armchairs and lots of wood . . . wood trim on the sofa arms, wood side tables and coffee tables, and lots of miscellaneous knickknacks on bookshelves and other horizontal surfaces. It wasn't Kiki's house anymore. How would I find her now?

I traveled to the hospital where Mike was a doctor and found him in an office with his nameplate on the door. He was sitting at a desk shuffling papers. He looked . . . different. And there was a ring on his left hand. Had he and Kiki tied the knot and moved? My only option was to wait and hitch a ride with him when he went home. I sat quietly until he packed up his briefcase and we took the elevator to the garage. Slipping into the backseat of his BMW, I patted the seat beside me for Brandy. He leaped in and curled up on the seat, but quickly remembered riding in a car, and it took a moment for him to calm down from the excitement of once again going for a ride, then he sat on my lap so he could look out the window, something he had loved to do when he was alive. I wished I could roll down the window so he could stick his head out. No matter. He still had a big doggie grin on his face.

A thought occurred to me. What if it wasn't Kiki that Mike had married? I'd been so sure they were perfect together.

And then we were pulling into the driveway of a stately house on a quiet tree-lined street of other stately houses. We waited for the garage door to rise, and I followed him into the house.

I heard Kiki's footsteps the instant we were inside, and, sure enough, she appeared at his side with a big smile and a welcome-home kiss.

Wait a minute... Kiki was pregnant? I mean, *really* pregnant. Like ready to give birth right there in the kitchen.

I felt so happy for her. What I wouldn't give to bear-hug her. For a moment, it seemed as if she could feel something and she glanced around the room with a quizzical look on her face, but she didn't see me.

Like I'd been able to project my energy at her so she could see me, I was also able to cloak my energy, which is what I chose to do. I didn't want to disrupt their lives again. Kiki would want to figure out a way to get that light back for me. But she had a different priority now. A family. And then, another surprise. A small blond toddler waddled into the kitchen and wrapped his arms around Kiki's legs, and she knelt down to ruffle his hair and kiss the top of his head. Yeah. I wouldn't interfere in her warm, happy life.

How long had I been sitting on that dock, oblivious to life moving on around me?

Chapter 38

Roz's shop was quiet when I arrived in her front room. No sounds of clients speaking excitedly about what they hoped was waiting for them around the corner. I stuck my head through the beaded curtains that separated the entry from her reading room. Roz's back was to me as she prepared a cup of tea, and my heart clenched when I saw streaks of gray in her flaming red hair. The world had moved on as I ignored its passing.

I saw her stiffen and heard her softly whisper, "Laurel," and she turned and looked right at me. I guess my cloaking powers didn't extend to her. She rushed forward as if to hug me but stopped just short.

"What are . . . why are you here?"

I could hardly bring myself to answer as tears filled my eyes, and I felt huge sobs trying to burst from my chest.

"Honey, what happened? Where's Teddy?" Her eyes were warm with concern. Unlike the old, salty Roz. Had she softened with age?

I . . . I didn't get to cross over. We saw the light, and Teddy stepped through, but . . . It was hard to talk about. Roz waited silently for me to continue. I gestured to Brandy, sitting on the floor looking up at me adoringly. *Can you see him?*

She peered at the spot I indicated for a moment and smiled. "I can."

I took a deep breath. *He was my best friend when I was a child. When the light appeared and we could see all our dearly departed loved ones waiting for us, Brandy couldn't control his exuberance and rushed out and jumped up on me, so I let go of Teddy's hand and picked up Brandy, and . . . and . . . and the light went away.*

Her lips tightened and she indicated her round reading table. "Sit."

I floated into the chair opposite the one she took.

"That's a bad break." She held up her hand to stop me from thinking she was minimizing my plight. "I know you're devastated. All you wanted was to move on, and you didn't get to."

I patted my lap, and Brandy jumped up into it. I didn't have the energy to respond.

Roz looked at Brandy thoughtfully. "You know, maybe it wasn't an accident. Your dog might have been sent out to distract you."

Why? Why would they do that to me?

"We can't know that. It's a question for the ages. But I don't think there are accidents."

I hugged Brandy and kissed his head. *It doesn't really matter now.*

"Where have you been all this time?" Roz asked then. "It's been, what, five years? Why haven't you gotten in touch with us?"

I've been nowhere. I guess I've been sitting on the dock since the doorway closed. I didn't have the heart to do anything but grieve. Then one day I saw Brandy waiting oh-so-patiently for me to acknowledge him and give him some love and decided to kick my stupor to the curb.

"Did you see Kiki and Mike?"

I saw them . . . but they didn't see me. I didn't let them.

"You know Kiki would *love* to see you again," Roz said.

I know. But she has a family now, with kids and a husband. I can't tear her away from that. You know she'd want to help me find the light again. I can't let her do that.

"You're a good person, Laurel Palmer. But maybe you should—"

It's better this way. Let her remember the happy me who was about to cross over. I want her to have good memories of me, and not worry about what will become of me.

"But you let me see you . . . "

I didn't. Not really. I tried to cloak my energy so you wouldn't know I was here, but with your psychic superpowers you saw me anyway.

Roz laughed. "Superpowers. Hah! Why did you come here then?"

I just wanted to know that my friends were okay and had good lives. I can see that Kiki does. Do you, Roz?

"No complaints. I'm content with my life. No giant ups, but no big downs either. Business is about the same, slow and spotty, but I have a pension from my late husband so I'm okay in that regard. Oh, and I'm dating a little bit."

Is he a good guy?

"I don't think he'll push me down the stairs or anything," she said with a wink. "No offense."

I giggled. *Not offended.*

"What are you going to do now?" she asked. "Is there anything I can do?"

I don't know the answer to either question. I don't know how to get the light back, but maybe it'll remember it left me behind and come back for me. And I seriously doubt you have the answer to my dilemma. So, I guess I'll just be wandering the earth . . . Brandy and I will be wandering the earth. At least I have him, so I'm not alone.

I lifted Brandy down from my lap and stood. *I just wanted to check on you. I miss you. If it weren't for you and Kiki, and Mike . . . well, at least Teddy found peace. Now I have to look for mine.*

I wiped a tear from my eye and Roz teared up, too.

So, what happened with Ethan? Did he get off scot-free? I asked, *or did—*

"Hopefully, the bastard will be spending the next twenty-five-to-life making license plates or carving shivs out of potatoes. Or whatever they do in there. His lawyers are appealing." She smiled. "Kiki, Mike and I attended the trial. We had quite a celebration when the guilty verdict came in." She fiddled with one of the bangles on her wrist before looking up at me. "Your parents were there every day. Kiki introduced me to them. I wanted so badly to tell them you were okay, but since you'd passed over and couldn't back me up, I would have sounded like a crazy person. They didn't need that."

I'm so sorry they had to go through that. Through any of this. Did they look like they were okay?

"Not really. Your death really hit them hard. As you would expect. Maybe with time . . . "

How do you ever get over the death of your only child?

"You don't. Unfortunately." She paused. "Are you going to visit them?

I . . . I'm not sure. I don't know if I can bear it.

"It's up to you, but it might give you some peace of mind."

I gave a sad laugh. *I'm sure Brandy would love to see them.*

"By the way, Ethan's appeal hearing is the day after tomorrow."

I felt apprehensive at the thought he might wiggle out of the sentence. *That doesn't make me happy, but I suppose it's not unexpected. Of course, he'd do everything he could to beat the charges. Are you going?*

"I don't think so. The actual trial was hard enough. There's nothing more we can do. I don't think Kiki will want to be any more involved than she already was, but I'll go if you want me to." She paused. "I'm sure your parents will be there, however. Will you be?"

Probably not. I don't care what happens to him anymore. But I felt a tug when she asked if I was going. Like a nudge to my brain almost pushing me toward the courthouse.

You don't need to be at the hearing. You've done enough for me.

"Besides, the appeal is for Teddy's murder, not yours."

So, he didn't try to appeal his conviction for killing me?

Roz wouldn't meet my eyes. "He never went to trial for your murder."

What? But—

"I'm sorry, Laurel. The police looked into it, but they decided they didn't have enough evidence to try him for it."

You mean he got away with it? That's not fair. He killed me. I couldn't stop the tears that gathered in my eyes.

"You're right. It's not fair. But you should find comfort in knowing that he's in prison and, with any luck, will be for a long, long time."

Small comfort. I don't know what to do now.

"Think on it. You'll know what you need to do."

I nodded and gave her an air hug.

She put on a brave face. "If you need me, you come back, okay? Anytime."

I gave her one last sad smile. *I'll never forget you, Roz.*

Chapter 39

Whoa. That was emotional. And troubling. Ethan got away with my murder. What if he gets away with Teddy's, too? It was out of my hands, but it still dragged at my brain. I wondered if it really did matter to me what happened to Ethan. Would I have failed if he went free?

It was painful to leave again after seeing Roz, but I couldn't spend eternity haunting her. She'd get tired of me hanging around after a while. And I had places to be.

As if…

I let Brandy run around outside the shop, nose to the ground hoping for an aromatic doggie scent, but finally called him to me and I willed us back to the dock. Ethan's boat was gone, and another opulent yacht, named "Sky's the Limit," was anchored in our old spot. I supposed Ethan had no use for it since he was in prison, and he may have had to sell it to pay his legal bills.

I needed to think about what my next steps should be. I finally gave into the certainty nibbling at my brain that I needed to see my parents one last time. Maybe I could give them some small measure of comfort, even if they didn't know I was there. I didn't go right away, though. It took a little while for me to build up the courage to view their grief in person.

When my emotions were under control, I motioned to Brandy, and he trotted up with his red leash in his mouth. I snapped it on and willed us to the kitchen of my parents' home. I knew I would find them there.

The familiar lightness was missing. There had always been something warm and enveloping when I sat in that kitchen, my dad with a cup of coffee and the newspaper spread out on the table, my mother bustling around loading the dishwasher or wiping down the counter. She was a bustler.

But a heavy feeling had settled over the cheery kitchen and those in it. My parents sat quietly at the table, no lively, engaged light in their eyes, untouched coffee and an unfolded newspaper sitting forlornly in front of them. Even Beau looked dejected, curled up on the floor at my mother's feet.

Beau lifted his head and sniffed the air when Brandy and I appeared in the kitchen, and a low growl formed in his throat. My mother looked at him in surprise.

"Beau, what's wrong? What are you growling at?"

Beau whined and scooted backward as Brandy approached for a sniff. He barked sharply and ran from the room. Brandy gazed up at me and whined for a different reason, not understanding why his new dog friend had run away before they could play. And he couldn't understand why the two people who'd been part of his family for years weren't paying any attention to him.

"That was odd," my mom said. My dad looked over to where Beau had last been and shrugged his shoulders.

And that was that. Neither could muster enough interest to try to figure out what had caused Beau to act so strangely. I leaned against the kitchen doorjamb and watched two sad people who existed in a pool of sorrow.

I approached my mother and wrapped her in my arms. She stiffened for a moment, and reached up as if to pat my hand, closing her eyes and smiling a small sad smile. Then she seemed to startle and sat up straight, pulling her shoulders up to her ears.

"You okay?" my father asked. "What's wrong?"

"Oh, I'm sure it's nothing. But . . . I could swear I felt . . . it felt like Laurel was here."

"That's nonsense," he said.

"You're probably right, dear." But she picked up her coffee for a sip and seemed just a little lighter.

I brushed my lips against my dad's cheek, and, for an instant, he looked around, and there was a glimmer of life in his eyes. I threw my arms around him and kissed the top of his head, then backed away as he waved at the air. I laughed and felt a tiny bit better.

Chapter 40

We could travel. I have all the time in the world. We could go to Paris. Or Jackson Hole! I love the Tetons and Yellowstone. And I wouldn't have to worry about bears anymore. It would have been fun to go with Teddy, but Brandy would have to do.

Brandy cracked me up. He carried his leash in his mouth when we'd go for a walk. I don't know where he got it from, but whenever I acted like I was ready to go somewhere, it appeared in his mouth, then disappeared again when we were done. I'd gamely hook it onto his red collar. And then he'd go ballistic, jumping up and down and pulling on the leash. Just like he used to do.

I snapped on the leash and willed us to Jackson Lake Lodge, directly onto the back terrace of the lodge which overlooks Jackson Lake and the big meadow where you could sometimes see moose and elk, maybe a bear or two. Ethan and I stayed there once when we were first married, and I never forgot how incredibly beautiful it was. Photo ops everywhere I looked. I'm not letting bad feelings about Ethan spoil the view.

The Grand Tetons provided a breathtaking view from the lodge's great room. Not that I had any breath to take.

I think it was summer when Teddy and I were together before he slipped into the light. It must be late fall now. I couldn't feel it, but there was a chill in the air. I knew from the way the lodge visitors were clutching their coats tightly around themselves. There was snow on the Tetons . . . of course, there usually was.

Two words: Unbridled Joy. That's what I saw as I watched Brandy pounce and race and gambol about the huge meadow stretching between Jackson Lake Lodge and the Tetons, head thrown back, ears flying. There was a group of dark specks quite a way out from us, too far to tell what they were, so I picked Brandy up and willed us to a spot near the specks, which turned out to be elk grazing. Brandy couldn't contain himself and wriggled to get out of my arms. He jumped up and down and spun in a circle anxious to explore and zoomed into the midst of the herd, barking excitedly at a particularly large elk with an impressive rack of antlers.

As Brandy slid to a stop at its feet, the elk froze and took several steps back, bellowing an alarm to the herd that caused them to spin and race from the meadow. Brandy chased after them, barking his little head off, but his short legs were no match for the long limbs of the elk.

He trotted back to me once he was convinced he'd never catch them, and licked my hand when I bent down to pick him up.

That was fun, wasn't it, sweetie? I kissed the top of his curly head and hugged him to my chest, then willed us back to the verandah. I sat on a bench with Brandy in my lap, allowing myself the luxury of basking in the grandeur spread out before me.

This might be the most beautiful place on earth.

Chapter 41

As I let my mind wander, a thought popped into my head, and I knew what my next step should be. The one place that might have answers.

There were no guarantees this would lead to the answer I was looking for, but it was the best I could come up with.

Come on, sweetie. Let's go. Brandy's leash immediately appeared in his mouth, and I snapped it onto his collar. We walked through the lobby of the lodge and out the front door, on our way to what I hoped would be the solution to my problem.

It must have been freezing at Niagara Falls. All the tourists sported puffy coats and warm scarves and knit caps pulled over their ears. I held Brandy up and pointed. *Niagara Falls, Brandy! I bet you didn't think you'd ever see that, did you?*

Mist from the roaring falls was heavy in the air, and droplets hung from the tips of Brandy's fur, and my hair as well. Brandy didn't have the patience to rest quietly in my arms and revel in the beauty of the tons of cascading water, and he wiggled to get down and move on.

I held onto the leash and let Brandy wander to the extent the leash allowed him. Resting my arms on the railing, I basked in the view of the wonder that was Niagara Falls at night. I wanted to feel, to remember, being here with Teddy. This was where we'd kissed the first time, where it all started with us. Both love and sadness washed over me. I felt the loss of him deep in my soul, and my tears were indistinguishable from the mist of the falls. When I finally let go of the grief, I willed us to my ultimate destination, Lily Dale.

· · ·

A feeling of peace settled over me as I wandered the quiet streets of Lily Dale, which were empty of people until morning. We made our way to the small green cottage where Susie Twilight lived and sat in one of the chairs on her porch where customers waited their turn for a psychic reading, to be ready as soon as we heard signs of life from inside.

I ruffled Brandy's fur. *I hope she can help us, sweetie.* He looked up at me with adoring eyes and reached up to lick my face. *I love you*, I said. If I didn't have Brandy, I don't think I could have faced going on after Teddy left. I couldn't blame Brandy for being so happy to see me, and me being so happy to see him, that we got distracted and missed the bright, shiny train as it pulled out of the station.

Ghosts don't really sleep, but we can get lost in contemplation, our minds wandering back to special moments and special people. It helps pass the time.

When I heard sounds from inside, Brandy and I floated into Susie's kitchen, where she was brewing coffee.

"I wondered if I'd see you again," she said without looking around.

How did you know it was me? I asked.

"Each spirit has a certain energy that emanates from it. A unique energy. And you have one of the most determined energies I've run across." She hesitated. "I don't feel your young man with you."

That's because he's not here. Just like you said.

"I'm sorry. I wish I hadn't been right." She carried her mug to the small wooden table in the kitchen and sat down. "Please," she gestured, "join me."

I slipped into the chair opposite her, and Brandy hopped into my lap.

"Who's your friend?" Susie asked.

I sighed. *This is Brandy. He was my dog when I was a child.*

"I'm confused. How did he find you?"

Teddy and I . . . Teddy was my friend . . . we managed to take care of our earthly business and were ready to cross over. The light came for us and we could see our loved ones inside. Brandy was there and, when he saw me, he rushed out and jumped up on me. I was surprised and, when I let go of Teddy's hand to scoop my dog up for a hug, the light went away. Brandy and I were left behind.

It was Susie's turn to sigh. "What a tragic story. So, it's just you and Brandy now?"

Yes.

She rubbed her face. "Is there something I can do for you?"

I don't know, but you're my last hope. Can you call the light back?

"No. I don't think it works that way. It comes when it's ready."

But it left us behind. Does it even know it left us behind?

"Sweetie, I don't have all the answers. I don't know how the light knows to come."

But you could try, couldn't you? Maybe ask your friends?

"Here's the thing. The spirits we see, well, they don't come to us. A family member comes to us and asks us to contact their departed loved one. Those spirits are connected to their loved ones, so they arrive with the person. We're just a conduit between the living and the dead. You're different. I've told my friends about you and your friend, and they've oohed and aahhed, but none of them has had that experience."

But the light . . . surely you've sent some of those spirits into the light, haven't you?

Susie just looked at me, an expression of compassion on her face. She opened her mouth to speak, but then closed it again. She reached out as if to take my hand but drew it back. "I'm so sorry."

I set Brandy down on the floor and stood. *I'm sorry to have bothered you.*

I gathered Brandy's leash in my hand and started for the door.

"Wait," she said.

I turned back. *What?*

"It's possible you're still here because you have more to learn before you cross over."

I don't even know what that means. As far as I know, I've learned all my all lessons. I was a good person while I was alive. Okay, after marrying Ethan I was wealthy, but I gave to charities and was still kind and generous and loyal and honest. I don't need to apologize to anyone or figure out how to be better. I don't mean for that to sound egotistical. I just don't understand what else there is for me to learn.

She picked up her mug. "It's also possible that Brandy was meant to separate you from Teddy. That the light leaving wasn't a mistake, but a plan."

Brandy wouldn't . . . he loves me.

"Of course he does. I don't know that's what happened." Her eyes were soft as she watched me. "You know, even if he were part of a bigger plan for you, he didn't betray you. He loves you. And if you were meant to go into the light with Teddy, the light would have waited for you. But it makes me wonder. Is there any unfinished business you need to attend to?"

*No, I—*Ethan's upcoming appeal had been on my mind since I'd seen Roz. But that wouldn't be the reason I couldn't leave, would it?

"What were you going to say?" Susie asked.

Just . . . my husband. He was convicted of Teddy's murder, but he's appealing that. He didn't get tried for mine. Could that be—

"Maybe you need to confront him. That might fall under 'unfinished business,' right?"

They left me behind because of that? It seemed so unfair.

She shook her head sadly. "I don't know. I don't have all the answers. I'm sorry. I wish I could be of more help."

I nodded back at her. *Thanks for at least hearing me out. I hope you don't see me again. No offense.*

"None taken. Good luck."

She'd given me something to think about. As I'd told her, I didn't think there was any unfinished business left to do. Maybe Ethan *was* the key. I made the decision right then to go to the hearing.

Chapter 42

The courtroom was sparsely populated. Up front was the prosecutor's side and across the aisle Ethan's team. Ethan sat next to his expensive lawyer, looking just a tiny bit less than smug. And not nearly as put together in that orange jumpsuit. I guess his attorney didn't get permission for him to wear a suit. There were scattered spectators, and my parents, sitting side by side in the second row, were among them. I saw several press people and some looky-loos. The judge banged his gavel and called the hearing to order.

I was barely aware of anyone except my parents, whose faces were drawn and haunted. They held hands and silently waited for the trial to start. My Aunt Lizzie sat next to my dad. Apparently, Ethan's appeal concerned prosecutorial misconduct. Something about errors that occurred in the first trial. I'd missed that trial, so I didn't know if any errors were made or not.

I slid onto the bench next to my mom and put my hand over hers. I felt her tense and look around the courtroom. I didn't know if my presence was comforting to her or more painful.

I glared at the back of Ethan's head. It would crush my parents if he beat the rap. Listen to me and my bad guy lingo.

I wasn't sure why I'd bothered to come to the hearing. I was too wrapped up in my parents' grief to pay much attention to the legal bantering. Until Ethan took the stand. I couldn't believe it as I watched him blithely proclaim his innocence and how his life had fallen apart after the death of his beloved wife, and that my death was just a tragic accident.

My parents both stiffened and I could feel their anger. And I felt mine growing as well. He wasn't going to get away with this.

I glared at him, and white-hot anger congealed my energy around me. I burned with bitterness, not for myself, but for the hell he'd put my parents through. He had to pay, or I'd never rest.

I stood and walked toward him and could tell the instant he saw me. His face went white, and he stuttered, "You . . . you."

Surprise! I bet you didn't expect to see me again, did you, Ethan? I could have laughed at the shock in his eyes, but there was nothing funny about any of this.

There was blood in my hair and soaking my dress, just the way it had as my body lay at the foot of the stairs. I thought it was a nice touch when I let it drip onto the floor of the courtroom in a gruesome way. His attorney was trying to get his attention, but that particular attention was focused solely on me.

You're not going to get away with what you did to me and Teddy. I'll make sure of it, even if the law doesn't. I smiled and floated toward him.

He was sputtering. When I was right in front of the witness box, I reached out my hands, blood dripping from my fingers, as if to grab him. He shrank back, waving his arms in front of him. His voice was high and wobbly as he screamed, "Get away from me!"

His attorney was freaking out, and the judge was banging his gavel, but Ethan wasn't aware of anyone but me.

"You can't be here, Laurel. You're *dead*." His eyes were big and wild. "I killed you!"

There was a gasp in the courtroom. My parents stood and hugged each other. The judge banged his gavel again and Ethan's lawyer objected.

"You're dead. *I killed you*!" Ethan repeated over and over, shielding his face protectively with his arms.

I'm going to heaven now, I said. *And you won't be going there.* I grinned at him as nastily as I could manage. *Well, that's up to God, of course, but he doesn't look too kindly on murderers.*

I smiled coldly as he was led from the witness stand, his eyes still on me. He didn't even notice Brandy growling and snapping at his heels. There was commotion in the courtroom following Ethan's confession, but it didn't matter to me. My parents had crumpled on the bench and my mother was crying softly as my dad held her.

"I thought I felt her here," my mom said through her sobs. "It was like she was holding my hand. But that's not possible, is it?"

"I don't think so, dear," my dad replied.

"Then why was Ethan talking to her?"

"His guilty conscience must have driven him to think he saw her," my dad said. "I'm glad if that was it. I hope she haunts him for the rest of his life."

They stood to go. Should I let them know I was really here? It was now or never. Instead, I stepped aside and watched them walk past me and out of the courtroom. A single tear slid down my cheek as they disappeared through the doors. I couldn't still be there for them even if I allowed them to see me. I couldn't appear to them and say that I'd been watching over them and then vanish. It would only leave them with questions they wouldn't be able to answer. It was for the best that I let them go.

Once the courtroom was empty, I sank down on the front bench and let out a sigh. Brandy, who was always at my side, sensed my mood change and whined at me. Yep. I was still here. Nothing had changed. Even though no light appeared for me, I was glad I'd come to the hearing. It had felt good to confront Ethan and know he'd never get over seeing my ghost.

At least I still had Brandy. I grabbed his leash and stood to leave the courtroom.

Laurel.

I thought I heard my name, but that was ridiculous. No one knew I was here.

Laurel, I heard again and stopped in my tracks. It was Teddy's voice.

I spun around and had to shield my eyes from the bright light hovering in front of the judge's bench. As my eyes adjusted, I saw Teddy holding out his hand to me.

This time I didn't wait. I dropped the leash and rushed into Teddy's arms, barely aware of Brandy at my heels.

The light came back for me. I'd never felt such love. It was omnipresent. Teddy and I held each other tightly, and over his shoulder I saw other spirits of my dearly departed waiting to greet me.

Welcome home, Teddy said.

And the light closed.

· THE END ·

Acknowledgments

There are so many people I have to thank. My sisters Sheila Baldwin and Michelle Hutton selflessly read through more than one draft of the manuscript and pointed out things I missed. My nephew, Chris Hutton, offered technical and creative assistance and actually came up with the name, although I think he meant it as a joke, but I loved it immediately and knew I wanted it to be the title of my book. I thought it was perfect! Thanks, Chris! My friend, Viki Lycksell, did a read-through and offered advice. Always appreciated! For a spiritual technicality, I consulted renowned medium Susan Grau, who walked me through what my ghost Laurel Palmer would need to do to get into Heaven.

My thanks also to Acorn Publishing, and the Acorn team, Jessica Therrien and Holly Kammier, who paved my path to publication. My editor, best-selling author Elaine Viets, offered kind words of encouragement along with her critical review. It's exciting to bring another of my novels to fruition, and I have high hopes that readers will love it as much as I do.

If you liked "The Continuing Adventures of Laurel Palmer," I would greatly appreciate it if you would consider leaving a review for me. As always, thanks to everyone who does choose to leave me a review. Those just might tempt someone to read my books! And, who knows? With enough reviews, maybe I could make a few bestseller lists!

Thanks again for sticking with me!

www.ingramcontent.com/pod-product-compliance
Lightning Source LLC
Chambersburg PA
CBHW030520310726
48979CB00010B/1747/J